The Army Air Force cadet returns home.

The whole world was golden with forsythia in bloom that noontime when Bill walked me home for lunch. He'd come off the morning train with just time to see Mom first. His uniform buttons sparked sunlight, and there was a little strut in his step. I rode all the way home on the wings of my hero. So did Scooter, as far as his house.

When Bill and I got home, Mom had all our favorites. Toasted cheese sandwiches and tomato soup. A pie was in the oven.

Bill was only home for a few days before he had to report for training. On Saturday he went out to Dad's station, and I tagged along. I shadowed him the whole time, trying to match his stride and memorize him for later.

ALSO BY RICHARD PECK

RICHARD PECK

On the WINGS of HEROES

PUFFIN BOOKS

PUFFIN BOOKS

Published by the Penguin Group

Penguin Young Readers Group, 345 Hudson Street, New York, New York 10014, U.S.A.

Penguin Group (Canada), 90 Eglinton Avenue East, Suite 700, Toronto, Ontario, Canada M4P 2Y3

(a division of Pearson Penguin Canada Inc.)

Penguin Books Ltd, 80 Strand, London WC2R 0RL, England

Penguin Ireland, 25 St Stephen's Green, Dublin 2, Ireland

(a division of Penguin Books Ltd)

Penguin Group (Australia), 250 Camberwell Road, Camberwell, Victoria 3124, Australia

(a division of Pearson Australia Group Pty Ltd)

Penguin Books India Pvt Ltd, 11 Community Centre,

Panchsheel Park, New Delhi - 110 017, India

Penguin Group (NZ), 67 Apollo Drive, Rosedale, North Shore 0632, New Zealand

(a division of Pearson New Zealand Ltd)

Penguin Books (South Africa) (Pty) Ltd, 24 Sturdee Avenue,

Rosebank, Johannesburg 2196, South Africa

Registered Offices: Penguin Books Ltd, 80 Strand, London WC2R 0RL, England

First published in the United States of America by Dial Books,
a member of Penguin Group (USA) Inc., 2007
Published by Puffin Books, a division of Penguin Young Readers Group, 2008

1 3 5 7 9 10 8 6 4 2

THE LIBRARY OF CONGRESS HAS CATALOGED THE DIAL BOOKS EDITION AS FOLLOWS:

Peck, Richard, date.

On the wings of heroes / Richard Peck.

p.   cm.

Summary: A boy in Illinois remembers the home-front years of World War II, especially his
two heroes—his brother in the Air Force and his father, who fought in the previous war.

ISBN: 978-0-8037-3081-6 (hc)

1. World War, 1939–1945—Illinois—Juvenile fiction.

[1. World War, 1939–1945—United States—Fiction.

2. Illinois—History—20th century—Fiction.] I. Title.

PZ7.P338Par 2007   [Fic]—dc22

Puffin Books ISBN 978-0-14-241204-6

Designed by Peonia Vázquez-D'Amico
Text set in Garamond 3

Printed in the United States of America

This book is for my sister, Cheryl

THE BOX ELDER TREE

Before the War . . .

. . . the evenings lingered longer, and it was always summer when it wasn't Halloween, or Christmas.

Long, lazy light reached between the houses, and the whole street played our version of hide-and-seek, called only by olly-olly-in-free and supper time.

Before I could keep up, I rode my brother's shoulders, hung in the crook of Dad's good arm. I rode them across the long shadows of afternoon, high over hedges, heading for home base, when our street was the world,

before the war,
when there wasn't a cloud in the sky.

Home Base . . .

. . . was a branchy box elder tree in front of the Hisers' house out by the curb. We could count on the Hisers not to mind when we pounded in from all directions to tag out on their tree. We plowed their sod when we skidded home, bled all over their front walk when we collided, knocked loose the latticework under their porch.

Big Cleve Runion, who was nineteen years old, lit once in the middle of their syringa bush in an explosion of sticks, and it didn't fill out again till after the war. But the Hisers had no kids and were getting on in years. They said they got a kick out of us. They were the rare grown-ups who liked noise, and Mr. Hiser was deaf.

5

Nobody was a stranger before the war. Everybody played. Dogs too, yapping at our heels. Dogs we didn't even know. They weren't locked up or walked in those days. They ran wild like the rest of us. Kids younger than I was were in the game, and big sweating galoots like Cleve. Kids from the other streets, and girls. Once in a while, dads, before they went to war or worked Sunday shifts. Always my dad.

We played to win. One time a big boy was it—Cleve or one of the Rogerses—and we took off for the alley to hunker behind the hollyhocks, my brother Bill and I. Our breathing was like dry leaves while a cracking voice yelled numbers into the tree. "Five, ten, fifteen, twenty."

When we heard in the distance, "Here I come, ready or not," Bill swung me up on his shoulders. We bobbed and weaved across a patchwork quilt of backyards, from one garbage can to another. Like magic, Dad was there by the Hisers' back drain spout.

In a Knute Rockne handoff, Bill passed me to him. I hung like a hammer off his belt. My feet danced in air, my head hung. There we came around the house, Dad pumping and wheezing, panting and red-faced with his bifocals fogging. Car keys and change rang in his pocket.

His timing was better than a kid's. Whoever was it never saw us coming, and it could have been Jinx Rogers, who played basketball on the starting five. I slapped the tree personally.

One time Dad dropped me. On a hot evening I oozed out of his slick arm and did a cartwheel, landing across the rocks around the Hisers' flower bed. The air went out of me, but there wasn't time to cry. Dad scooped me up and ran to the tree. I took giant strides in the air just above the grass, and we tagged in with seconds to spare.

Later, when I'd outgrown the crook of his arm, when Bill was away, Dad stayed in the game a little longer. He'd find another toddler to tote. Or he'd erupt, all on his own, a hundred and ninety pounds, out of the Hisers' thrashing bushes and swerve toward the tree. His work shoes slapped the bricks of the street before he could get himself stopped. But he always let himself get caught if he didn't have a kid in his arms.

"He's the biggest kid on the block," Mrs. Jewel Hiser said from her porch, over the spirea, "that Earl Bowman."

Smiley and Jewel Hiser . . .

. . . were country folks who'd retired into town when Hitler invaded Poland. Mrs. Hiser had seen newsreels of refugees fleeing the Nazis along rural roads, pushing all their belongings in baby carriages.

She believed the rumor that if we got into the war, there'd be no gas or tires. We'd all be trudging along on foot like the refugees. So the Hisers bought the second bungalow from the corner behind the box elder tree. There they settled into their porch swing to await invasion.

Mrs. Hiser said she saw World War Two coming before Roosevelt did. Way before. She'd never been easy in her mind since the *Hindenburg* blew up, which she said was a Sign. She was a great one for Signs and could describe the exploding *Hindenburg* like she'd been on it.

Passengers burning alive staggered on fleshless feet through its melting steel skeleton. Mrs. Hiser had a fine sense of doom and kept a scrapbook of clippings about automobile accidents and house fires.

Her tales were always worth hearing again, unless you were my mom, who said once was all she needed. The Hisers played to a full porch for the one about a nephew of hers who'd skidded on his sled. He shot under an International Harvester truck and scalped himself.

They were living history to me, the Hisers, older than Dad. Mr. Smiley Hiser drove a 1930 Essex. Mrs. Hiser had played piano for silent movies before talking pictures came in. She played by ear, whatever that meant, and could render any song as long as it wasn't new.

If you asked her for "Chattanooga Choo-Choo" or "Mairzy-Doates," she'd just look at you. But to show us what real music was, she'd spring out of the swing and slip indoors to her upright piano. We waited for the crack of her knuckles, then "Yes, We Have No Bananas" or "Too Much Mustard" or "If You Knew Suzy" or even "Papa Get a Hammer, There's a Fly on Baby's Head" pounded out in the night.

Both Hisers were musical, though Mr. Hiser was deaf. When they sang "Just a Song at Twilight" in close harmony, they held hands. Which amazed me in people of their years.

On hot nights Mrs. Hiser remembered a boy cousin of hers who got lost in the Blizzard of 1896, between the cow barn and the house. He froze nearly to death and shook so bad he bit off the tip of his tongue.

"How did you get him to stop shaking?" somebody always had to ask.

"We never did," Mrs. Hiser recalled. "We just tied him to the churn and made butter."

We hung on her words and waited for the cackle of her laugh. She kept a lace handkerchief down the vee of her housedress for wiping under her glasses because she seemed to be laughing or crying most of the time.

"Get her to tell you about Jimmy Johnson and the cornpicker again," Dad mentioned to me one night after supper. I didn't ask why.

You could hear a pin drop whenever Mrs. Hiser ran that one past us. It was a ghost story, and she'd seen one.

"You want to hear that again?" she said, later on in the evening, closer to lightning-bug time.

Scooter was on hand that night, and the Bixby sisters, and me, naturally. We perched in a row on the porch rail under the hanging ferns. The story was about the early days of mechanized farming when the tractor took over from the team and the motorized cornpicker came in.

The cornpicker revolutionized farming, but it had a flaw. You wanted to be careful or it'd take your hand off. There was a generation of one-armed farmers because of it, so this was a story right up Mrs. Hiser's alley.

Mr. Jimmy Johnson was their country neighbor down in Moultrie County. He was a good farmer, but slow to adapt to modern ways. He bought himself a cornpicker, then lost a hand pulling stalks out of the snappers because he'd neglected to shut down the engine.

She could make you see that ripped-off hand vanishing into the chomping cornpicker. In some of her tellings it wrenched the whole arm off at the shoulder. Popped it off like a wishbone.

Mr. Johnson had stood there in shock, watching the cornpicker eat his arm, along with his shirtsleeve and the button on his cuff. In all her tellings, blood went everywhere. Mr. Johnson left a trail of it up to the road, where he died in a drainage ditch. The Bixby girls clung to each other. Scooter's profile was freckled green chalk in the twilight.

"Everybody turned out for the funeral," Mrs. Hiser remembered, and Mr. Hiser nodded. "Will I ever forget Jimmy laid out in his coffin? The blacksmith carved an artificial arm to fill out his sleeve, with a hook at the end. Crossed on his chest was his good hand and the hook."

We quaked on the railing as the coffin lid closed, and I was real alert now.

There was more to come, as we knew. How well Mrs. Hiser remembered a certain night weeks later. From her country kitchen door she saw a strange and far-off light, down the picked rows of corn in the late Mr. Jimmy Johnson's field.

Now she was on her back step, dishrag in hand, drawn by the eerie, changing glow. It was like a bobbing lantern, but different. She'd stood transfixed beside her cream separator.

By now I was pretty sure Dad was under the porch, or in the spirea. He had to be around here somewhere, about to improve on the story and scare us all senseless. I was trying my darnedest to be ready.

"Then I saw Jimmy Johnson out there in his field," Mrs. Hiser said, almost too quiet for Mr. Hiser to hear, "real as the living man, with a lantern in his only hand."

I listened hard for Dad, but he seemed to miss his moment.

"He held the lantern high, and he was looking everywhere," Mrs. Hiser said. "Then I heard him myself, a voice that moaned like the windpump.

"*Where's . . . my . . . hand?*' the ghost of Jimmy Johnson cried.

"*Where's . . . my—*'"

Beside her, Mr. Hiser turned to Mrs. Hiser. Scared himself even after all these tellings, he reached for her. Her hand reached back, to close over . . . a wooden arm with a hook at the end.

Her head bobbed like a blue jay when she saw this inhuman thing in her lap. The hook gleamed. She gasped, and her corsets creaked like a ship in a storm. When her scream split the night, porch lights winked on.

Jimmy Johnson's cold hook had appeared in her lap in place of Mr. Hiser's hand. Mrs. Hiser rocketed out of the swing. When she came down, her lace-up shoes hit the floor hard enough to drive tacks. Jimmy Johnson's artificial arm, back from the grave with hook attached, rumbled off across the uneven porch. Mr. Hiser set his heels to keep from pitching out of the swing and bent double with laughter. Dad had to be doing the same, a house away.

We never heard the cornpicker story again, though we always asked for it.

I'd noticed Dad at his workbench in our basement, turning an old table leg on his lathe, fixing a coat hook to it with a wood screw. It was similar to the one that reached for Mrs. Hiser. How Mr. Hiser hid it till the right moment, I didn't know. He must have sat on it there as they swung, together in the swing.

The Street . . .

. . . played hide-and-seek till the first frost when the leaves fell from our hiding places. We heard the Hisers' stories and heard them again until a chill in the air sent the storytellers inside. Then came Halloween. Something in Dad lived from one Halloween to the next.

For one of my first ones he'd carved a pumpkin big enough for several candles. It leered from our porch larger than life, beside the front door. I remember the smell of scorched pumpkin pulp. The rest is common knowledge.

Bunches of boys roamed Halloween night, big boys from somewhere on the far side of the park. They didn't trick-or-treat or wear costumes, not even sheets. They were there to soap your windows, shave your cat, pull siding off your house, do something nasty down your mailbox, knock over pumpkins. Dad couldn't wait.

The spirea bushes around our front porch closed over his head when darkness fell. Dad had lit the pumpkin, prepared the porch, filled the buckets at his feet down among the spirea roots. Now he waited. No gang of boys could match his planning, his patience.

They came, drawn like moths. It looked so easy. They grouped down by the box elder and sprang from tree to tree, sprinting across our yard. They were quiet for boys as they brushed past the spirea on their way up our steps. The one in the lead carried a baseball bat to flatten the pumpkin. Ganging closer, they crested the porch. Then their world went awry.

The porch floor rattled like hailstones under their feet. The leader's boots went out from under him. His bat took a wild swing at nothing. He fell flat on his back, measuring his length on a floor thick with ball bearings.

It was a hard fall, and the wind shrieked out of him too late to save the others. They dropped in every direction as the ball bearings spun like steel marbles under them and cascaded down the steps. The boys behind took the full weight of the ones ahead. They grabbed and grappled and fell in a gaggle down the noisy Niagara of the steps.

When they were in a heap at the bottom, Dad rose out of the dark and the spirea to let fly with the first bucket of water. Still, they couldn't find their feet, or words, and they were drenched. It was a cold night with a ring around the moon.

Their leader was still on the porch. He rolled off his back and whimpered as the ball bearings bore into his hands and knees. His arms skidded, his elbows bounced. Dad had another bucket just for him.

At last they grunted off across the yard, gathering speed. Their knicker legs were slick and clinging, and they were still running into each other, all their mischief forgotten. They didn't look back to see Dad there, sprouting out of the spirea, grinning like the pumpkin.

I got a bat out of it, not quite a Louisville Slugger, taller than I was. Years after, you could still find ball bearings, like rabbit droppings, down among the spirea roots.

The Last Halloween . . .

. . . before the war, Scooter Tomlinson and I went out trick-or-treating in masks one final time. Now that we were in Cub Scouts, we figured we were getting too old for this type of thing. We'd been at it for years, ringing doorbells in the dark, demanding our treats. Tootsie Rolls, Cracker Jack, home baking, all that booty before the war took the candy away, the sweetness.

I came home in the night, dodging shadows, whistling in the dark. The Pluto mask was parked on top of my head. I was swinging a sack of treats.

The Hisers' box elder tree was the center of our universe. The other landmark was the 1928 Packard coupe parked out in front of our house. It was Dad's fishing car. He drove it to work, one of the biggest, heaviest cars ever built. It was thirteen years old and looked older, and no particular color now. The front bumper was a two-by-six plank. When Dad fired it up every morning, people awoke four blocks away.

The Packard bulked at the curb, darker than night, empty as a looted tomb. But I knew better. I climbed up on the running board and peered into the open window. "Dad?"

He was in there behind the wheel, pulled back in the shadows, smaller than his regular size. The window on his side was down too.

A sacred Halloween ritual was pinning horns. If a Halloweener could get into a car, he'd jam one end of a stick into the horn on the steering wheel and the other end into the back of the seat. Then he'd run like the devil while the car owner had to come out and unstick the horn before the battery ran down. Car horns went off all over town. One went off right then, over on Summit. Dad was waiting for business, and the windows were down for bait.

He was also out there in the cold and the dark, watching for me, waiting for me to come home.

"Climb in, Davy," he said. "Keep down."

I leaned into the old hunting jacket he wore over his Phillips 66 uniform. The car smelled like a grease pit and dead pheasants.

"Get anything good?" he said, and I offered the sack. The diamond in his Masonic ring glinted when he rummaged for a taste.

"Fudge," he said, and spat it out his side window. He wouldn't swallow chocolate. The army had issued the soldiers bars of bitter chocolate to keep them awake, in France, back in his war. He wouldn't eat anything they'd fed him in the army.

"Whose?" he asked.

"Old Lady Graves." She was an old crab but baked especially for Halloween.

She also lived on the far side of West Main Street. Still, I wasn't afraid to mention that Scooter and I'd crossed it. The two of us crossing a thundering truck route after dark, not looking both ways, in masks, wasn't the kind of thing that troubled Dad. You didn't have to watch every word.

I slid one hand into the game pocket on his hunting coat and sat on the other. You could see your breath. The sky was powdered with stars, and again there was a ring around the moon. Dad had already told me that as a kid he'd lain on top of a haystack to watch Halley's comet.

I began to nod off. He didn't. All the porch lights were out now. Mom had gone to bed.

Sometimes I could hear Dad thinking, and it was pretty much always about my brother Bill. He was gone by then, down in St. Louis, taking the Civil Aviation Administration course at Lambert Field. War was raging out in the world, other places. Bill was nearly nineteen. That's what was on Dad's mind.

He nudged me. "Get way down."

He could hear a Halloweener a mile off, behind a building. He was easing down till his back was flat on the car seat. The old cracked leather wheezed beneath us. His Phillips 66 cap edged forward over his face. I could get all the way under the glove box without knocking off my Pluto mask.

It felt like we were down there several days. Then came the fall of a foot in the leaves along the curb. A faceless figure was coming up behind us, past our back bumper. He'd have a stick in his hand, the right length. A chill rippled down my spine. But Dad was there, much of him arranged around the steering column.

The figure stepped up to the driver's side and found the window down. He couldn't believe his luck, and sighed. He leaned in with his stick.

Dad's hand shot up from nowhere and grabbed a wrist. The stick snapped, and a terrified voice yelled, "Mama!" before he thought.

Dad sat up, never letting go. "What can I do for you, son?" he asked, friendly enough.

The figure couldn't think. He was trying to twist out of Dad's grip, and failing. "Y-y-you can turn me loose." But that wasn't going to happen.

I stayed where I was under the glove box. It was bound to be one of the Rogers boys, and I didn't want to be a witness. It wouldn't be Jinx, who kept his nose clean with his senior-year basketball season coming up. But there were several other Rogerses, all bad dreams.

20

"I wasn't gonna do nothin'," the twisting Rogers said, overlooking the stick in Dad's lap.

"Hop on the running board," Dad said, still gripping him with a fist the size of a ham. The Packard's running board was a foot wide, plenty of room to ride. With his free hand, Dad turned the key, jerked the choke. The Packard roared alive. Lights in bedroom windows went on. People may have thought it was morning.

Dad switched on the headlights, and we drove off down the street. I was sitting up, tucked behind Dad's shoulder.

The Rogerses lived halfway down. Dad swung into their driveway and pulled up by the porch. We'd have sounded like a Sherman tank coming through their living room wall. The porch light went on, and Old Man Leland Rogers came out in his pajamas. He squinted through the screen wire.

"Earl?" he said. "Which one you got?"

"Which one you missing, Leland?" Dad said around the squirming boy.

"I wouldn't miss any of them if they was all in the reformatory," Old Man Rogers said. "But I thought I had 'em counted." He was chewing a cold cigar. "Don't let him go till I get there."

Old Man Rogers unlatched the screen door and tramped down to the car in his bedroom shoes. Dad handed the boy over. I sneaked a peek, and it was their eighth grader, Homer. He was flapping his hand, trying to get the circulation back into it.

"You fool," Old Man Rogers said to Homer, and pushed him up the porch steps.

So now that everybody was accounted for and home safe, we backed out of the Rogerses' drive and drove up the slumbering street, Dad and I, my hand in his pocket.

The Dwindling Year . . .

. . . slipped away from there. We raked one last time, got the storm windows up, and it was December.

After church, we always ate our Sunday dinners in the dining room: old hen and slick dumplings dinners.

One Sunday we were tucking in when we heard an awful racket outside and a hammering on our back door. Mrs. Hiser was yelling through the glass for us to turn on the radio and take cover. They'd bombed Pearl Harbor and could be heading here.

Something hit Dad hard. He pushed his plate away like it was army food. Mom reached out for Bill's empty chair. And all the world before the war went up in far-off smoke and oil burning on water.

REMEMBER
PEARL HARBOR

Only Fifteen Shopping Days . . .

. . . were left till that Christmas of 1941. Crowds bustled. Shelves cleared. The window of the Curio Shop on East Prairie Avenue was heaped high with broken dishes, torn fans, ripped-up paper lanterns. They'd wrecked all their Made-in-Japan merchandise and made a display of it that drew a crowd.

Scooter and I looked, but it was something in the window of Black's Hardware that pulled us back every Saturday, to see if it was still there.

A Schwinn bicycle stood in the window. A solitary Schwinn, casual on its kickstand, sharp as a knife. Two-toned cream and crimson with a headlight like a tiny torpedo. An artificial squirrel tail dyed red, white, and blue hung off the back fender under the reflector. I couldn't look at the thing without tearing up. You could have played those chrome spokes like a harp. And look at the tread on those tires.

It was the last Schwinn in town, and maybe the whole country, for the duration. The duration was the new wartime word, and you heard it all day long, like the song "Remember Pearl Harbor," on the radio, over and over. The duration meant for however long the war would last.

I'd been wanting a two-wheeler for a year and thought I could handle that Schwinn, though it was full-sized and weighed thirty pounds. I thought I was long enough in the leg and had the arms for it, almost. Never mind that I didn't know how to ride a bike.

I didn't expect to get it for Christmas, and didn't. It was twice what bikes cost, and the last one on earth. Scooter and I checked on that Schwinn faithfully, knowing that one Saturday it wouldn't be there.

I pictured the kid who'd get it, some rich kid from up on Moreland Heights. I saw him in new Boy Scout shoes and salt-and-pepper knickers and a chin-strap helmet with goggles, swooping down a curving road with that patriotic squirrel tail standing out behind. I saw the easy arcs he made from ditch to ditch. He'd be a little older than we were, a year or two older.

We didn't know what to expect out of Christmas this year. Scooter usually did pretty well for presents. He already had his Chem-Craft chemistry set. We'd had our first fire with it, burning a circle out of the insulation on the Tomlinsons' basement ceiling.

The stink bomb we'd built to go under Old Lady Graves's back step had gone off too soon, in Scooter's arms. I threw up the minute I smelled him, and his mom made him strip naked in their yard. She hosed him down and burned his shirt in a leaf drum. But that was last summer after his birthday.

One December Saturday when we checked, Black's window was empty, and the Schwinn was gone.

Dad brought home a tree standing up out of the Packard's rumble seat. People said there'd be no trees next Christmas and no string of lights when these burned out. Mom baked all Bill's favorites. Dad rolled out peanut brittle on a marble dresser top. People said that next year there wouldn't be enough sugar for Christmas baking.

But this one still smelled like the real thing: pine needles and nutmeg, Vicks and something just coming out of the oven in a long pan. And Bill was home. "That's Christmas enough for me," Mom murmured.

We untangled the strings of tree lights, Bill and I, stretching them through the house. He could stick the star on top without stretching. But then he and Dad had hung the moon.

Bill was home from St. Louis with a full-length topcoat and his aeronautics textbooks. Bill wanted to fly, and he was taxiing for takeoff already.

He and Dad were down in the basement on Christmas Eve, puttering on mysterious business while Mom kept me busy. When Bill came upstairs, wiping grease off his hands, the kitchen radio was playing "Stardust." Bill swept Mom away from the sink, and they danced, turning around the kitchen like it was the Alhambra Ballroom and Mom was his date. Her forehead was shiny, and her eyes were shining. She still held a dish towel that hung down from his shoulder. They danced until the radio began to play "Remember Pearl Harbor," and Mom switched it off.

Bill slept in the big front room upstairs. Dad had divided the attic in two and boxed in the rooms under the eaves. I had the little one at the back. We didn't get a lot of heat up here. On nights this cold I wore mittens and a cap to bed.

You could talk between the rooms. The wall was beaverboard, and we left the door open. From his bed, Bill said, "Davy? You remember to hang up your stocking?"

No answer from me. I was too old to hang up a stocking, as we both knew.

"What did you get me?" Bill inquired because it was a known fact that I couldn't keep a secret.

"A pen wiper," I said. "Pen wipers for everybody. We made them in school."

"Miss Mossman?" Bill said, naming my teacher. He'd had her. "A pen wiper's good," he said. "I'll keep it on my desk and take it with me. Wherever."

Silence then. Silent night.

"What did you get me?" I asked, and my breath puffed a cloud. I hoped for his high school letter sweater, Cardinal Red. He'd lettered in track. I'd go in his closet and try it on a lot. It hit me just above the ankle.

"You get anything for me?" I asked in the dark because he was drifting off.

"Socks," he mumbled, "underwear."

"Oh," I said. I turned over once, and it was morning.

A Stack-of-Pancakes Morning . . .

. . . with Staley's syrup and bacon popping in the pan. I woke up to the jangle of the sleigh bells on the old leather harness Dad had always rung to make me think Santa was just leaving.

Dad wouldn't give up on the bells.

Downstairs, the tree lights were on, though daylight poured in. All the Made-in-Japan glass balls on the tree glittered in their prewar way. We were all there in our bathrobes.

But right in front of the tree was a bicycle. The kickstand dug into the living room rug.

It took me a second because the room went blurry. But it was a bike, painted a gloss black with a thin silver stripe. Not quite a Schwinn, but not that heavy—leaner, faster-looking. I didn't want to move or say anything. I might wake up.

Then I saw it was Bill's old bike. The tires were a little smooth. But the paint job was showroom fresh, hardly dry. And where did those chrome fenders, front and back, come from? They were new, or off some other bike. Dad must have looked around for them. And that stitched-leather seat? The handlebars had seized up with rust long ago, but now they were sanded down, and the bell was new, and the grips. Hanging down below the rear reflector was a squirrel tail. A real one, off a squirrel.

"Is it mine?" I said.

And they said yes.

We got through the morning and the other presents. I handed out the pen wipers. Finally the four of us were outside on the driveway with the bike. It was cold, but there was no ice underfoot.

If this had been a real dream, I'd have climbed on and ridden away down the drive, down the street, into the world without a wobble. I'd been on bikes before, other people's and junior-size. But I'd fallen right off and crusted both knees.

This bike of mine was full-size. Somebody had built up the pedals with wood chunks.

Dad held the handlebars while I climbed on. The seat fit that part of me like a glove. The balls of my feet grazed the built-up pedals. But it felt like I was up a tree, and the concrete on the drive looked far away and hard. Bill stood a bike's-length away, but not near enough. Dad gave a push, the front wheel went sideways, and over I went.

Over and over. But we kept at it. I was wringing wet under my layers, and they were working overtime not to laugh. But we stuck to it. I was going to find the balance, learn to ride. It was part of my present, and the day. Back and forth I wobbled, from one pair of big hands to another. Mom watched, dancing out of danger in that graceful way she had, because I went in every direction.

Just for a flash I found it. The wheels and I aligned. I zipped past Bill and rode the length of the house before I sprawled off and the bike fell on me. And that hurt, but I didn't let on. By the time they got to me, I was up and climbing, stumbling over the chain guard.

Then it worked for sure. I'd started back by the garage, and I was still on and steering when I came down the slope of the drive to the street. There were no hand brakes then. You back-pedaled to stop. I forgot and barreled across the street into the Blanchards' driveway before I fell off.

But I was like the Wright Brothers, both of them, at Kittyhawk. I'd flown this far.

I turned the bike, alone here on this side of the street. I was sucking wind, blowing steam. And there coming up the street was Scooter, red-faced in a stocking cap.

He was on the Schwinn from Black's window.

On and off it. And his dad was running along behind, picking him up, putting him on again. But Scooter was biking too, almost, and on that brand-new Schwinn with the two-tone paint job and the headlight like a tiny torpedo. He usually did pretty well for presents.

And it was all right. It was swell. We both had bikes, and mine was Bill's.

Miss Mossman . . .

. . . did her best to bring World War Two into our classroom. At first it was uphill work this far behind the lines. Still, several of us hoped they'd bomb the school before we got to decimals. Also, Miss Mossman wasn't any good at geography. Scooter was and took over the classroom map and the box of pins. On the Monday after Pearl Harbor, he'd put in a pin to show Hawaii. Before Christmas, he'd put a pin in Germany.

By the end of winter, a poster hung over Miss Mossman's desk, showing an aircraft carrier sinking, under the words

LOOSE LIPS SINK SHIPS

If we knew any military secrets, we weren't to tell anybody who could be a fifth-columnist, which was the wartime word for spy. I took this personally since I couldn't keep a secret.

Every Thursday we brought as many dimes as we had for pink War Savings Stamps to stick in a booklet. When you had eighteen dollars and seventy cents, you traded the booklet for a War Bond. It would mature in ten years and be worth twenty-five dollars.

"I hope you *children* mature in ten years," Miss Mossman said.

Toward the end of the winter when they started rationing rubber, she saw her chance to get us into the war. Rubber was the first thing to go because the place it came from was behind enemy lines now. Scooter put a pin in the Malay Peninsula.

Guidelines from the Office of Price Administration, the OPA, told kids to bring in all old rubber items to a point of central collection. We'd be competing with other schools. Miss Mossman said anything could help the war effort, even rubber doormats.

"Not ours," Mom said.

LaVerne Bixby brought her mother's dishwashing gloves. Duane Hemple brought in all seven of his Seven Dwarf rubber statuettes, which he was a little old for. Somebody threw in a pair of handlebar grips, which reminded me to keep mine with me when I wasn't on my bike. People brought in a mess of rubber.

One morning just before the Pledge of Allegiance, Walter Meece, who was slow, shook out a sack of something into our collection corner.

On the stroke of eleven, a big woman loomed up at the window of our door. She rapped once and stalked in. Miss Mossman was in the middle of telling us something and stopped. It was Mrs. Meece, Walter's mother, clutching her big pocketbook.

"Where's the stuff?" she said over us to Miss Mossman. But she could see our rubber pile from there. She started up an aisle, brushing desks on both sides. Walter got down in his seat, thinking she was coming after him. But she turned at the front of the room, sharply past Miss Mossman.

When she bent over our collection, a silence strangled us. She grunted and sorted through—galoshes, hot water bottles, bathing caps, a played-out garden hose. She had on a big hat. When she found what she was after, she held it up.

One of the girls screamed.

Mrs. Meece was holding a rubber girdle, huge. Hers.

She shook it at Miss Mossman, who'd turned to stone. "I've got an Eastern Star luncheon today," Mrs. Meece said, "and I have to fight my way into this thing first."

Out she stalked with the loose ends of her girdle flapping outside her pocketbook.

Later that day somebody heard Miss Mossman out in the hall talking to the principal, Miss Enid Howe. "We're collecting nothing else in my classroom," Miss Mossman said. "*Nothing*. I don't care. Fire me."

But Miss Howe didn't.

The Phillips 66 Station . . .

. . . that Dad ran across town in the North End was on a different planet from our leafy street. Now that his helper Charlie had been drafted, he was down to part-timers. Dad was back and forth from the pumps to the lift, running himself ragged.

I told him I'd be glad to drop out of school and help, at least for the duration. I could pump gas and read the tire gauge. If I could get the hood up, I could check the oil. But Dad said we'd talk about it when I was bigger than the dipstick. I'd be out there on Saturdays sometimes, getting underfoot, pretending to work.

Dad ran the station like a club where old codgers hung out on the pump island, complaining and remembering. And on cold days he let paperboys roll their newspapers in the station, out of the weather. You had to be twelve for a paper route, and they were a tough twelve. They wore no socks with their knickers, and they wrote things in ink on their arms. I overheard vocabulary from them I didn't know what to do with.

I was there the Saturday after the OPA issued a new order. A car owner with more than five tires was to turn in any extras to his local gas station. They'd clamped a freeze on tire sales. Now you needed a certificate from the Ration Board, and it wasn't easy. The government made it hard to get a new tire, but they wanted your old one.

Mr. Smiley Hiser drove across town to turn in an extra spare to Dad personally. His old Essex sedan with pull-down window shades stood square out by the pumps. I shook out the squeegee to wash down his windshield. We gave full service.

Dad ducked out from under a car on the lift when Mr. Hiser rolled his extra spare across the pavement.

"Smiley," Dad said, "where are you going to find another tire for an Essex when you need your next one?"

"Say what?" Mr. Hiser said, cupping an ear.

"Take your tire home, man," Dad boomed. "We'll all be riding on rims before this war's over."

"They say it'll be over by Christmas," Mr. Hiser said.

"They said that last time," Dad remarked.

A long car pulled up at the pumps. A bulky guy in a belted coat got out and swaggered over. He had Big Shot written all over him. "Say, listen, buddy," he said to Dad, "give me a Firestone for a Cadillac."

Dad looked him over. Eight or so tires still hung on the lubritorium wall.

"I've got a certificate from the Ration Board," the big shot said, "if that's what's worrying you." He flipped a wallet out of his overcoat. A whole page of precious tire certificates unfolded like a road map.

"I can't help you," Dad said.

The big shot sighed and put his certificates away. He reached out with something wrinkled sticking out of his fat fist. A twenty-dollar bill. I'd never seen one.

Dad didn't seem to see it now. "You heard me say I can't help you."

I dropped back over by the pumps.

"Don't waste my time." The big shot jerked a thumb at the tire wall. "You've got one left."

"It's earmarked for a regular customer," Dad said, which couldn't be exactly right because he didn't have a regular Cadillac customer.

I dipped the squeegee into soapy water. To reach the Cadillac's windshield, I'd have to walk up the front fender, which the big shot wouldn't like. But he was busy. I could barely reach across the window on the driver's side.

"This war's a real opportunity for you little guys to throw your weight around, isn't it? For the first time in your life."

Nobody talked to Dad like that.

"Maybe you don't know who I am," the big shot said. He was standing too close, in Dad's face.

"Maybe I better not find out." Dad's right hand clenched. It wasn't his good hand, but this guy wouldn't know that. I almost fell off the fender from looking back. The big shot's ears had gone an ugly color. When he turned around, I jumped down off the fender. Dad's work shoe rang on the pavement behind him, and the big shot made a kind of skip. He piled in the Cadillac and thundered out onto Division Street.

Mr. Hiser blinked from Cadillac exhaust. "What did he say he wanted?"

"More than his share," Dad said.

"Wonder who he was."

"The Water Commissioner," Dad said.

I was beside them now, and Dad wasn't grinning, so you wouldn't even recognize him. I held up something to show them, and now they both blinked. It was the Cadillac's wiper blade, off the driver's side, because nobody ought to talk to my dad like that.

"It could have worked loose anyway," I said, "sooner or later."

"Son," Dad said, "that's not what we mean by full service." But his hand was working over his mouth, and he was grinning behind it. That's all I wanted.

"Say what?" Mr. Hiser said, cupping an ear.

Eight-to-Five Orphans . . .

. . . was our name for all the new kids flocking into school now from all over. They brought their lunch in buckets because their mothers were working in the new war plants, so they couldn't go home for noon. Behind Miss Mossman's desk, posters showed women with big arms working on the assembly line with planes streaking overhead:

KEEP 'EM FLYING

the posters said, and

RELEASE A MAN TO FIGHT

Before the war, nobody'd been a stranger. Now everybody was, practically. We were jammed in all the way over to the radiators. The new kids dressed funny and talked funny. Some of them were rough customers for this end of town. Three of the girls were.

Now a bucket of sand and a shovel stood next to Miss Mossman's wastebasket to put out incendiary bombs. She said they could burn you to a crisp. According to her, the Enemy was waiting for the war plants to get into full production. Then the sky above us would be black with bombers releasing their payloads on us.

A wall chart from the Office of Civilian Defense, the OCD, showed how to duck and cover, grab your knees, tuck your head. Miss Mossman said to expect drills regularly. But we only had one, as it turned out.

"When I blow this whistle three times, it could be a practice. It could be the real thing. Don't tarry to find out," she said. "Get under your desks."

They might not be incendiary bombs. The Germans had used poison gas before and might again. If anybody smelled it, he was supposed to yell "GAS!" We were to have handkerchiefs to stuff in our mouths so a bomb blast wouldn't knock our teeth out. For the poison gas, we'd need them to cover our noses.

Late one morning, Miss Mossman let fly with three blasts on her whistle. We peeled out of our seats and hunkered under our desks. Heads tucked, mouths full of handkerchief. Happy to. Anything for a change. They were the old-time desks with inkwells and scrolly iron sides, bolted to the floor.

We all seemed to fit under there, even Hoyt Albers, who was the biggest boy. Even Beverly C., an eight-to-five orphan who sat across from me. I wondered if she would.

Beverly C. was junior-high big and then some. Big and shapeless, like a boulder with hair. We wondered if she was even our age, and I still won't give her full name for fear she'll find me.

Under our desks we were all quiet for once. But then Mervyn Krebs hollered out, "GAS!"

He must have spat out his handkerchief. We all did, and heads banged the undersides of desks all over the room. This was our first real scare, and I got a whiff of something pretty bad myself.

Then we got busy working our handkerchiefs over our noses in those close quarters. Above us, Miss Mossman sighed.

"Walter Meece," she said, "come up."

Walter said it wasn't him, but he got up out of the desk in front of Mervyn's and wandered up to the front of the room. Miss Mossman wrote him a restroom pass, and then we listened to Walter tripping over the bucket and shovel on his way out.

When we scrambled up after the all-clear, Beverly didn't. She was wedged in there tight as a tick, with parts of her bulging through the scrollwork sides. There wasn't a cubic inch under her desk that wasn't Beverly. She tried to move, but she was down there for the duration.

When she saw, Miss Mossman moaned. "Oh, sweet heaven help me." She too was afraid of Beverly.

The room went dead. People got to work folding up their handkerchiefs. You didn't laugh at Beverly, and people were scared they would. Or even smile. She had two sidekicks, a pair of eight-to-five stooges, Doreen R. and Janis W. They didn't fight at Beverly's weight, but they packed a wallop. Everybody owed them a dime apiece on War Stamp Thursday. They were on their feet, monitoring, checking to see if anybody laughed. They could spot a smirk rows away.

I grinned. Before I could help it. The sight of big Beverly, almost a solid block in the shape of her space, made me grin before I thought.

Doreen saw and pointed at me across the room, which was doom enough. But Beverly herself saw. Over her hunched shoulder one of her squinty eyes saw me through the iron curlicues. Her incendiary stare burned me to a crisp.

"You, Davy Bowman," Beverly said, unblinking. She never called you by name. "At noon you'll be picking up your teeth all over the school yard. You won't have nothing left to grin with. And you'll wonder where your nose went."

I heard her every word. She was only muffled by her shoulder. She didn't own a handkerchief, as you could see by her sleeve.

I fried through eternity while Miss Mossman and four boys tried to pry Beverly out of her desk. Why should I help? When she was free, she was going to kill me. And nobody to stop her. None of the boys would come up against her and Doreen and Janis. Scooter himself sat quietly at his desk, gazing out at a robin on the windowsill.

Somebody had to go for the janitor. If I'd been sent, I wouldn't come back. When he turned up with a wrench, he found Beverly crated for shipping. I barely noticed when he unbolted her desk and the ink from her well went everywhere. We dipped pens then. Ballpoints didn't come in till after the war. I wondered if I could outrun Beverly, and how that would look. I thought about the fire escape.

Now she was out, expanding in the aisle on legs like kegs. She was big enough to pick up a mule. While the janitor bolted her desk back to the floor, she looked down at me under a single heavy brow. And she made a fist the size of Dad's.

I just sat there.

Then sweet heaven helped me.

It was nearly noon when somebody knocked on the classroom door. We all looked—anything to take our minds off Beverly. Miss Mossman blocked our view when she opened the door. Then her arms went out.

"Is that Billy Bowman," she cried, "all grown up?"

It was. My brother Bill was there. It was the cavalry sent to save me in the nick of time. I heard galloping hooves, flags flapping, a bugle.

Bill was there to take me home for lunch, a miracle almost too big to believe. I chanced a glance back at Beverly.

You wouldn't know her. She was some other girl. She gazed up at my brother. Her squinty eyes were round, batting. Her mouth was open. Her grubby hand stole up to touch her awful hair. And I saw my troubles were over, at least for now.

"Who zat?" she whispered like a prayer.

"My brother," I said.

And looking good. Taller and handsomer than ever. It must be the uniform. He was an Army Air Force Cadet.

The Whole World Was Golden . . .

. . . with forsythia in bloom that noontime when Bill walked me home for lunch. He'd come off the morning train with just time to see Mom first. His uniform buttons sparked sunlight, and there was a little strut in his step. I rode all the way home on the wings of my hero. So did Scooter, as far as his house.

When Bill and I got home, Mom had all our favorites. Toasted cheese sandwiches and tomato soup. A pie was in the oven.

Bill was only home for a few days before he had to report for training. On Saturday he went out to Dad's station, and

I tagged along. I shadowed him the whole time, trying to match his stride and memorize him for later.

In weather this good all the oldsters in the North End hung out at the station. Every old retired railroader and trucker sat out on the pump island, swapping lies, spouting chaw. When they saw Bill in his uniform, it put them in mind of San Juan Hill and Teddy Roosevelt.

"After they get to that age," Dad said, "they were all Rough Riders." They looked up at Bill between them and the sun, and their old eyes watered. One glimpse at Dad's eyes, and I saw he was memorizing Bill too.

We went out to dinner, the four of us, on Bill's last night. The band at the Blue Mill played "To Be Specific, It's Our Pacific." When they saw Bill, they struck up "Nothing Can Stop the Army Air Corps."

After we were in bed, I said to him through the wall, "How long till you'll be shooting down planes and releasing payloads, that type of thing?"

"The training takes most of a year," Bill said, "though they're speeding things up."

"So you'll be home again, before . . ."

"One more time," Bill said.

He went the next morning when I was at school. I knew the time the train left and watched it on the clock. When I got home, all the gear was gone from his room, and his bed was made with military corners.

That was the first night I went upstairs without being told. Then I thrashed in the sheets, sat on the windowsill, thrashed in the sheets some more. Bill was sitting up that night on the train, and tomorrow night and the night after that. I counted miles instead of sheep.

When I was just drifting off, some sound from his room stirred me, some small sound. At first I thought Bill was back, home from a date or a night game—something. Now I was wide awake, eyes peeled in the dark.

There was nothing to hear now. Still, somebody was in Bill's room. Why didn't it scare me under my bed?

I eased the sheet back and slid out. Stepping over the squeaky floorboard, I waited and watched in the doorway between my room and his.

The streetlamp from out on the corner threw a shape of light across the angled wall. There was the dark triangle of a Fighting Illini pennant, and the shape of somebody sitting on Bill's bed. Slumped there.

A hand rested on the pillow, and the streetlamp caught the diamond glint in the Masonic ring. Dad was sitting on Bill's bed. There was enough light to see he had Bill's letter sweater pulled over his shoulders. Dad, sitting there in the dark, where Bill had been.

Scooter Put a Pin in Midway Island . . .

. . . and school was out. The radio said the tide in the Pacific was beginning to turn.

Two days into summer, and we forgot where school was. But it was too quiet, this summer, though we'd waited and waited. The world emptied out. Jinx Rogers had gone from commencement to basic training at Camp Leonard Wood, Missouri. Big Cleve Runion was up at Great Lakes.

Bill was out in Santa Ana, California, writing back:

> *. . . It's all book-learning and bodybuilding so far. We run everywhere instead of walking,*

and Joe DiMaggio himself leads our calisthenics. In nine heavy weeks of math, we're going from the times table to trig . . .

Dad worked a longer day. Everybody was waiting for gas to be rationed, but he said it wouldn't be till after the election. Only kids played hide-and-seek now, so Scooter and I didn't. We played some catch in the street, fed each other some fastballs. But I was used to three-corner with Dad and Bill, and the Packard for a backstop. August was on the way already, and there wasn't even a state fair, not for the duration.

When we got tired of nothing happening, Scooter and I set off to collect enough of whatever it took to win the war.

"Let's get this war over with," Scooter said. "I'm sick of it."

"GAS!" I said to liven things up, and we rummaged around for handkerchiefs we naturally didn't have.

Then we went off collecting. We were tired of rubber, but we'd take anything that wasn't nailed down. Especially scrap metal because if you turned in twenty-five pounds of it, the Varsity Theater would give you a free ticket for a Saturday matinee.

We started with our own street, skipping the Hisers, who always used everything up. They were laying out a victory garden that ran back to the alley. By the end of the summer, rows of sweet corn rustled like open country, and there were tomatoes enough for all. Mrs. Hiser put up fifty-two bottles of her own ketchup, one for every week, in recycled

Royal Crown Cola bottles. The summer smelled like spiced tomatoes simmering.

We had our Number One ration books now, after the big sugar panic of the spring. Sugar was down to a trickle, so Kool-Aid was out. Everything on the table was going to be rationed sooner or later, canned goods because of the tin—everything. The Hisers were ready.

Mr. Hiser said he'd retired from retirement. He was in bib overalls again and his Purina Chows cap.

"You boys are welcome to do some digging and weeding," he told us, so Scooter and I got busy collecting scrap farther down the street.

The oldest house dated from before bungalows, like a house in the country before the town crept up. An old man lived there alone. Mr. Stonecypher. And if any house in town was haunted, here it was. So Scooter and I dared each other to begin at Mr. Stonecypher's. It sounded swell till we got there.

We pulled our Radio Flyer wagons around to the back. We'd tried hitching the wagons to our bikes, but that hadn't worked. "You knock."

"No. You."

The back door flew open, and we fell off the step and grabbed each other.

Mr. Stonecypher glared out. He looked like Father Time. "Stick 'em up," he said.

We stared.

"Whatcha want?" He had a voice like a gravel pit.

"WHAT HAVE YOU GOT?" Scooter yelled at him, really brave. "WE'RE COLLECTING STUFF FOR THE WAR EFFORT."

Mr. Stonecypher jerked. He had eyebrows like nests. "Quit yelling," he said. "I'm not deaf. That's Hiser."

"Tin cans?" Scooter said. Housewives were to soak off the labels, flatten the empty cans, and take them back to the store. So said the OPA. There was no housewife here, but Mr. Stonecypher looked like he ate straight from the can.

"Five thousand tin cans will make a shell casing," Scooter said like he knew. I let him do the talking.

"That a fact," Mr. Stonecypher said. "Don't stand in the door. Come on in. You're letting the flies out."

He didn't tell us to wipe our feet, and no wonder. We stuck fast to the kitchen floor. Everything was flaking or rusted out. It was fairly interesting, but only in daylight.

"Whatever you've got we'll take," Scooter said, all business. We were looking for metal because of the movie tickets, but whatever, even rubber. But not paper. Paper came later.

A brown picture of a young soldier in an old uniform hung in the living room. The place was so clearly haunted I couldn't believe it. Scooter spotted a wind-up Victrola with a gigantic brass horn. A load of scrap metal right there.

"How about that?" he asked Mr. Stonecypher, who was on our heels.

"Nothin' doin'," he said. "Them things is coming back."

"How about your basement?" Scooter said.

"Forget my basement. It's off-limits," Mr. Stonecypher said. "I keep my still down there. If you saw it, I'd have to rub you out."

A still was for making corn liquor. People made their own at home back in Prohibition times. We looked at him. Did he know Prohibition was over? His teeth clicked at us. "You can scout around the attic. I got a job for you up there."

A problem with old people, as we were to learn, was that they always had a job for you.

Down a dark hall, Mr. Stonecypher pulled a folding ladder out of the ceiling, and Scoot swarmed up. So I had to.

The eaves up there were clotted with dried wasps' nests. An old lightbulb with a pointed tip hung down. Scooter pulled its chain so we could see because there was only one pokey window over the front porch roof.

"See that winder?" Mr. Stonecypher's voice echoed up. "It's open a crack. Shut it for me. I don't want to get bats in my belfry."

Scooter stared at me with round eyes. *Too late*, he mouthed. But he banged the window down, which caused a lot of buzzing in the walls.

"How about these toys?" Scooter yelled down. An open box was heaped with really old cast-iron toys. A little touring car and a toy implement like a manure-spreader or something. Many things, small but heavy.

"Leave them."

We jumped. Mr. Stonecypher had followed us partway up the ladder. Only his eerie old head showed, like a skull on the attic floor.

"And keep clear of that trunk."

Over against the webbed eaves stood a hulking foot locker, stenciled with brown letters. "Don't mess with it, or I'll have to rub—"

"How about that?" Scooter pointed out the head of an old brass bed. A single bed, but tall. It was a couple of movie tickets right there.

"If you can get it down, you can have it," Mr. Stonecypher said, "and tell 'em to drop it directly on old Hirohito's head. And that'll do you." He vanished.

We worked for half an hour getting the brass bed loose and down the ladder in a shower of mouse droppings. It was about too much for us. We were at the back door now and heading for open country with it. Mr. Stonecypher was still on our heels, and his teeth were clicking like a Spanish dance. When we were outside, he said, "Here's some more metal for you."

He put out his old papery paw and dropped a dime into each of our hands. "And you ought to wear your Cub Scout uniforms, or something to make you look regulation. Ain't everybody as friendly as I am."

Then he banged the back door on us.

We'd sweated through our polo shirts, and the bed kept falling off the wagon.

"What do you think was in that trunk?" I asked Scooter.

"Mrs. Stonecypher," he said.

Dad Could See in the Dark . . .

. . . as any Halloweener could tell you. The Civil Defense issued him a white tin helmet and an armband with the striped diamond in a circle, and he was the street's air raid warden.

When the siren sounded, I supposed I'd be sitting home in the dark. But Mom handed me something, an armband with a striped diamond in a circle, homemade and the size to fit over my puny bicep. She was doing more sewing now. Clothes rationing was just around a couple of corners.

The armband wouldn't have fooled anybody, but it felt right. Behind us, Mom threw a towel over the radio to hide the orange light in the dial. They said the Luftwaffe could see a struck match from a mile up. At the door, she pulled on me. "Don't let your dad fall down. Watch out for him."

"Because he's the biggest kid on the block?" I said.

"No," Mom said. "Because he isn't."

Outside you couldn't see where the porch steps ended. The corner streetlight was off, and there wasn't a star in the sky, like they'd blacked out heaven. The Packard out at the curb could have been anything—a pile of lumber.

The Hisers' house next door was a black shape. Even the night birds seemed to be standing around on their branches, wondering what happened.

I kept next to Dad. We were to spot for any stray lights left on, and our beat was both sides of the street, from the park boundary at our end down to West Main.

The Hisers' porch swing squawked in the night. There was nothing to see out here, but they wouldn't have missed it. Dad flashed his red-bulbed light up at them.

"Earl?" Mr. Hiser spoke over the spirea. "Hitler was here, but he seen you coming."

The Hisers cackled.

Box elder roots had heaved the sidewalk, but Dad's foot knew that slab by heart, from hide-and-seek. A lot of people were on their porches. It was too hot inside, hotter than a Model T radiator, as Mrs. Hiser always said. Living room radios blared so that people could hear the WDZ rebroadcast of a Brooklyn Dodgers game. The Dodgers were enjoying a ten-and-a-half-game lead. You could follow the play from house to house. "There's the pitch . . . and it's low and outside . . .".

We were passing the Friedingers' place when I got the idea we were being followed. It was probably just being out in the dark, but I could feel it down my back. A shoe scraped behind us, and I leaned into Dad. I wasn't about to look around. A small rock got kicked.

We were even with the Bixbys' overgrown lilac bush. Dad edged me off the sidewalk. One sidestep, and we'd vanished into bush branches. My hand hooked Dad's belt. Twigs fingered my face. Somebody was coming along the sidewalk. A step, then a stumble. Somebody wondered where we'd gone. The night stood still.

A shape, small and gnomish, passed us, a reach away. We stepped out, Dad with me stuck to him. He flashed his red bulb on the follower.

Face glaring red in the dark, bug-eyed, Scooter shrieked.

He was scared out of his wits, but what did he expect? We were out here on official business, which he wasn't. Dad reached into his pants pocket. Was he going to cuff Scooter and run him in? Seemed fair.

Dad pulled something out and handed it over. "Here, Scoot," he said. "Try this for size." I saw in the red light it was a homemade armband like mine. Mom had sewn two of them. And it was okay. It was fine. Dad had another side, and Scooter took it.

We went on past the Rogerses' house, but we were safe enough with Dad here. That's when we saw our first light, beaming like a beacon down through tree limbs from an attic window. It was Mr. Stonecypher's. Scooter looked around Dad at me.

"Well, he's an old duffer," Dad said. "Who knows how long he's left that light burning."

Scooter and I happened to know. He looked around at me again. We'd forgotten to turn out the light when we'd brought the brass bed down, days and days ago. Weeks? Anyway, it had slipped our minds. We'd been busy.

"We'll wait," we said when Dad turned up the front walk, but he told us we were on duty. The Stonecypher porch crinkled with last year's leaves. Dad knocked, then pounded. The house was dark as pitch, except for the attic.

The door sprang open, and there etched against blackness was the ghostly Stonecypher shape.

"Keep them hands where I can see 'em," he greeted. Scooter and I shrank.

"Mr. Stonecypher," Dad said, pointing to the attic, "whose side are you on?"

"Who wants to know?" he rasped. "That you, Earl? Why you wearing a wash pan on your head? Better come on in before you get lost. They're havin' a blackout. And don't stand in the door. You'll let the flies out."

Scooter groaned. But we had to go in, and it was that same smell of old medicine inside. Dad said he was showing a light upstairs, though Mr. Stonecypher didn't think so. But when he pulled the ladder out of the hallway ceiling, light flooded down. He spotted Scooter and me, blinking. His old eyes narrowed, but his jaw clamped shut.

"I'll skin up there and turn it off," I said, helpful.

Scrambling up the ladder, I grabbed for the light chain. The box of ancient toys was still there. And the old trunk over in the eaves with the stenciled lettering. Then I was feeling my way back to the ladder past the trunk.

Mr. Stonecypher wasn't in a big hurry to see us leave. Now he hung in his front door.

"Earl, you tell me what this war's for when you find out," he said to Dad. "You tell me what the last one was for." The fire in his old eyes flared, but his head drooped. I could see in the dark now.

Dad put his hand out on Mr. Stonecypher's sloping shoulder. He kept it there, and Mr. Stonecypher put his face in his old hands. There was a bad, shaky sound like a sob.

"I wish I could tell you," Dad said in a voice half his size.

Mr. Stonecypher swallowed hard. "You got through it, Earl." He looked up, and his old face glistened. "You may have been roughed up, but you come through and come back and had your life and your boys."

"I did," Dad said, "but a lot of the best ones didn't make it."

Mr. Stonecypher turned in the door, and Dad's hand slipped away. Then the old, old man closed himself into his house, and you could feel him in there, in the dark.

We made the rest of our rounds, down to West Main, which was the truck route. The Civil Defense Auxiliary Police were directing the traffic that crawled along with just running lights. We headed back on Scooter's side of the street, Dad between us, bear-big in a night too dark for shadows.

"Dad, what did it mean? With Mr. Stonecypher?"

"He lost his son in the First World War," Dad said. "His only boy. He'd have been my age. Maybe younger."

We were by the Tomlinsons' front walk. "There's a trunk in his attic with letters on it," Scooter said.

"That'd be the foot locker they sent his boy's gear back home in," Dad said. "That's what he's got left."

We watched Scooter up to his porch. The all-clear sounded, and the world came back. The streetlamp on our corner showed us the way home. Lights in porch ceilings came on, buzzing fishbowls in yellow halos, all the way to ours.

"We're going to have to look out for Scooter," Dad said.

"How come?"

"His dad's taking up a commission in the navy."

"Scooter never said."

"Maybe he's not ready to," Dad said. And I remembered the snazzy Schwinn that Scooter got last Christmas. It could have been his dad already saying good-bye.

I leaned into my dad the rest of the way.

"When you're taller than I am," he said, "are you still going to stick this close to me?"

"Sure," I said. "Why not?" So he threw an arm around my spindly shoulder, and we went on home. Mom was pulling a towel off the Philco, and a song welled out: "When the Lights Go on Again All Over the World."

Now the Government Wanted Milkweed . . .

. . . to replace something called "kapok" from the Malay Peninsula. Milkweed was for stuffing in life jackets, to keep shipwrecked sailors afloat, or pilots who'd ditched at sea.

At the tag end of summer the stuff was bursting out of its pods along every country road, and Scooter and I wanted to be outdoors till the last second before school. We'd already scooped up enough scrap metal to get us into the Varsity Theater through all next year and into 1944.

Last summer the park was the size of our universe. But the bikes pushed out our boundaries. We fell off them and got crossways in traffic. I'd crashed down a culvert and sprung the frame on mine. But we'd been almost to Maroa and Mt. Zion on secondary roads. Sacks for the milkweed hung off our handlebars and caught the breeze.

We were out past Wyckles Corner one blazing morning so close to September you could smell school. There was milkweed, tangled with ragweed and goldenrod. We'd just bumped our bikes over a blue racer snake, dead in the road with a red smear where a car had run over its head.

Before Scooter got any ideas about tying the snake to his back fender, I wanted to put some distance between it and us. The road was ankle-deep in dust, so it was uphill pedaling the whole time.

Back in the fields stood a ruined old barn with a Red Pouch Tobacco sign flaking off its side. A falling-down barn and then an old sloping house. You could see daylight through both of them. Deep in weeds up by the house was a beat-up 1933 Chevy sedan with suicide doors. It had a license plate, but it looked pretty weary.

There was a mess of milkweed, but we liked the look of the spooky old barn. The doors were off it, and I thought we could see enough from out here in the lot. Snakes could be in there out of the sun, snakes with swaying heads. Copperheads. We looked inside, then looked again.

In the middle of the dirt floor were the remains of an ancient automobile, striped with sunlight, furred with dust. An old jalopy like the mummified corpse of a car in this rickety tomb of a barn.

"Neat," Scooter breathed, and walked his Schwinn inside. He parked it against a support beam, so I had to. A row of rusty rattraps hung webbed together down the post.

The car had been old when Packard built Dad's. Even the chicken droppings on it were older than we were. Wooden-spoke wheels. The tires were long gone, and everything had lived in it at one time or other: chickens, hogs—snakes, no doubt. The crank was still in the slot under the radiator.

Anything this historic had to be a treasure. Scooter smeared spit on the radiator cap, and the nickel winked—nickel, not chrome. He rubbed an emblem, and the faded letters read: PAN AMERICAN.

The hood was missing, and generations of animals had been nesting in there, living in messes of their—

"Something ate the roof," Scooter said, but the skeleton of it was there, like a ribby old umbrella. Scooter turned the latch, and the front door jumped off the car and smacked the dust of the floor. Then we were sitting on the front seats, leather oozing stuffing.

Scooter was behind the big wood steering wheel. The metal pedals stood high enough for his feet. Mine dangled because there wasn't much floor on my side. We sat there, pretending the missing motor was turning over, firing back through the tailpipe. Scooter geared down with the missing shift. We were two sports from another time, barreling down country roads, free as air, old enough to drive.

"There wasn't even a war then," Scooter said.

From the regulation canteens on our web belts we drank the last of our water. A breeze drifted through. It was breezier than a cane-bottom chair, as Mrs. Hiser would say. I dozed.

The barn turned into a covered bridge, also rickety, and we were thundering through it in our brand-new Pan American straight from the dealership. It was the days of yore, and the President of the United States was . . .

"Warren G. Harding," Scooter mumbled out of his own daydream. He reached to squeeze the invisible bulb on the missing horn. "Beep, beep," he sang out.

Soon after that, an explosion about busted my eardrums. Hail rattled the roof from a clear blue sky. Scooter peeled out of his side. I slid off my seat. We thought about rolling under the car, like school air raids. This could be the real thing.

"Scram!" Scooter yelled. "The barn could be coming down." And true, it was raining roofing.

We cut out, then pulled up short. A black shape stood in the barn door against the sunlight. The figure held a shotgun.

I may have screamed. Scooter did.

The hail on the roof had been buckshot out of the gun. I'd never been so scared, and dying this far behind the lines didn't seem fair.

"Well anyway you're not tramps," the figure said.

Our eyes adjusted. It was a dried-up woman with a face like a walnut. She'd lowered her blunderbuss. Had that just been a warning shot? The gun hung broken open in the crook of her wrinkled arm, like she'd been out hunting. Her skirt tails were in her boots. What century were we in?

"But boys in a barn are trouble enough," she said. "Start toward me."

My heart lurched, and I had to follow, keeping even with Scooter. "It was that Beep Beep of yours that gave us away," I muttered to him. His web belt was way bigger than Scooter's waist. It worked down over his knees as we walked, closer and closer to this old woman and the barrels on that shotgun, still smoking.

"Smoking?" she said. "Cornsilk in a dry barn?"

"N-n-no," we said.

"What's in those canteens?" she inquired. "Home brew? Rot gut? Corn liquor?"

"N-n-no," we said.

Scooter's belt wound down to his ankles, and his canteen settled in the dust.

"Town boys," she noticed. "What's your business in my barn?"

Scooter found his tongue. I'd left mine somewhere. "We're collecting milkweed for the war effort," he piped.

"Did you find much milkweed growing inside my barn?" She wore tortoiseshell spectacles, old as the car. Her magnified gaze crackled through them.

"We like your old automobile," Scooter said in a small voice.

"And you just make yourselves at home on other people's property?"

We pretty much did. We'd been in and out of other people's attics and basements all summer long, scouting for scrap. We didn't mention it.

"Up to the house." She nodded toward it. Scooter stepped out of his belt, and then we were on the porch, out of the sun—and options. A slop jar, covered, stood on the floor. The screen wire on the door billowed out.

"Inside," she said, parking her shotgun against the house, which was some relief.

Inside, hogs wouldn't have come as a surprise. But it was mostly stacks of books. Shelves with more books ran across the top of a closed door to another room. A kerosene lamp stood on a big table with a stack of newspapers and *Time* magazines. She'd been eating her lunch at one end, on oil-cloth, when she heard intruders in her barn.

"You. The talker," she said to Scooter. "What's your name?"

If she got our names, our gooses were cooked. "Scott W. Tomlinson," Scooter said. "Ma'am."

"And what do they call *you?*" She swiveled on a bony hip. Her dress was a feed sack.

". . . Davy."

"Bowman?" she said, but how did she know? Was she a witch? She looked it. Who was she?

"I am Eulalia Titus. Miss."

"Pleased to meet you," we lied softly.

She sent Scooter around the back of her house. She had a jar of something cooling down her well and told him to bring it. "And watch where you step. Snakes."

Scooter scooted. I could feel myself turning pale because of snakes in the vicinity.

"You better sit down," Miss Eulalia Titus said. "You may have had a touch of the sun."

She'd been reading a new book by Ernie Pyle, the great war correspondent. "You thought I was too far back in the sticks to know there's a war on," she said. So she read minds.

Scooter came back with a jar of buttermilk. Miss Titus poured out three cheese glasses. It was barely cool, and I hated buttermilk.

"I suppose you two are used to iceboxes," she remarked.

Actually, we were used to refrigerators.

The three of us fit around the end of the table. Miss Titus was small and stringy, though of course she could blow you away. Scooter's elbows were nowhere near the oilcloth, so he was minding his manners. A screen-wire dome among the books covered a tall cake with butter icing.

We three were knee to knee. Miss Titus had a little mustache. "Just so you know," she said, "that cake took two weeks' sugar ration."

"Sixteen ounces," Scooter said.

She gave him a look. "You're the sharpest tool in the shed, aren't you?"

He looked modest. Also, he had a buttermilk mustache. Miss Titus's was real.

"He's the smartest kid in our grade," I said, which was true.

Miss Titus stood up to cut three slices out of the cake. It was layer.

"Where's mine?"

A terrible voice came out of nowhere, or the grave.

"I said where's mine?"

Scooter froze. Every hair on my head stood up. If I'd had hair anywhere else, it would have stood up too. That voice was scarier than the gunfire, and where had it come from?

"All right, Mama!" Miss Titus pushed back from the table.

Mama? Miss Titus was the oldest woman in the United States. And she had a mama? Scooter smacked his forehead.

Miss Titus pushed a door open. Looking back at us, she said, "You think *I'm* mean."

We fidgeted. From the other room a voice like a crow cawing said, "Is it store-bought cake or homemade? Because I like store-bought."

Miss Titus sighed.

"Who's out there?" the voice demanded.

"Two owlhoots I cornered in the barn, Mama."

"What do they want?"

"They say they're collecting milkweed, but I think they're trying to steal Papa's automobile." Miss Titus looked back at us over her spectacles.

"Milkweed's a weed," came the aged voice, "and the auto's junk. Send them in here."

Oh no. Hadn't we been punished enough? Miss Titus pointed at us. We stumbled over and peered around the door. The other room was mostly bed, with a black-walnut headboard to the ceiling.

In that bed was a woman that time had forgot. She had a face like the Grand Canyon. She was bigger than Miss Titus, and somewhat balder.

She peered. "But they's little varmints."

Scooter sighed.

Miss Titus gave us a pair of pushes, and we were by the bed. The old lady leaned over to take a better gander at us. Strange smells wafted out of the bed. We were close enough to see all the craters in her nose.

"Guess how old I am."

We couldn't.

"I'm ninety-seven years old. Put that in your pipe and smoke it."

We just stood there.

"When you're old enough," she said, "are you going to fight for your country?"

We guessed so, we said, if the war lasted that long.

"What about your daddies?" Her old hand came up to stroke several moles and small chin growths.

"My dad fought in the last war," I said.

Silence. Then Scooter said, "My dad's in it. Shipping out from San Diego."

So he got it said finally. But it took this.

"We're waitin' on my brother," Miss Titus's mama said, turning her face to the wallpaper curling down the wall. "He writes and says when he gets back home he's goin' to furl his flags and forget about killin'. And the army ain't gettin' him back. They'd have to burn the woods and sift the ashes to find him. He plans to melt down his medals and throw his uniform on the fire."

Like my dad. He wouldn't even wear a brown suit, after all these years.

"And I ain't forgot about the cake," she said over our heads to Miss Titus.

That was it. We could go then. Miss Titus said she was going to see us off the property, to make sure. And just so we knew, next time she'd aim lower. She'd put a new part in our haircuts. Out on the porch I had to ask her. "Your mama's brother. Is he a lot . . . younger?"

"No, he was older," Miss Titus said. "He was with General Logan's 31st Illinois Volunteers. The Civil War, of course. She's worn his letters out, but she's waiting on him to come home now. It keeps her going."

From the porch she watched us off the place. The track down to the county road was one rock after another, so we walked our bikes. Then we were pedaling back toward town, the milkweed escaping out of our sacks, silky into the August afternoon.

"I don't know," Scooter said. "Maybe we're giving too much to the war effort."

He had a point. I kept pedaling. "But it was a swell old automobile."

"Way too historic for scrap," said Scooter.

We pedaled across Wyckles Corner without looking both ways. "The trouble with this war," Scooter said, "is the only people left at home are old as the hills and cranky as Old Nick."

My dad wasn't cranky as Old Nick, but how could I say so when his dad was gone? "The cake was good, though," I said, which Scooter agreed to.

A Teacher Shortage . . .

. . . raised our hopes, but this year school started on time. Our teacher was Miss Landis, and it looked like her first year on the job. She painted her legs light brown and drew a dark line up the backs for the seam because ladies' stockings had gone to war. Thirty-six pairs of nylons made a parachute, according to Scooter.

There was a diamond ring on Miss Landis's finger, and her soldier was overseas. Scooter put a pin in England to show her where. Though she was shaky on long division, he gave her some pointers. She was real pretty, which helped her with the boys and hurt her with the girls. Especially three of them.

In October Scooter pinned Guadalcanal as the war seemed to stall. The tide wasn't turning now. Bill was in flight school, writing from Bruce Field, Texas. He was practicing touch-and-go landings, and he'd be soloing pretty soon, before winter. War edged a little closer. Then it broke out in our classroom.

Miss Landis mentioned that she was going to inspect the state of our hands and nails starting tomorrow after the Pledge. Her hands and nails were nice. In fact, her manicure was better than her math.

Tomorrow came, and hands spread on desks as she started up and down the aisles. As luck would have it, Beverly C. sat across from me. There hulked big Beverly with her uncombed hair standing out like something gone to seed. People said you could see things moving in Beverly's scalp. I never looked.

As Miss Landis approached, Beverly made two big fists. Miss Landis hovered and made the mistake of tapping one of Beverly's big knuckles with a perfect fingertip.

"Lady, don't think about touchin' me," Beverly rumbled back in her throat. But she opened her fists just to show Miss Landis what she thought of the inspection. Her hands looked like she'd been stripping down an outboard motor and changing the oil on a truck. Her nails were chewed down to the half-moons.

Miss Landis started. "Oh dear," she said. "Beverly, honey, do you own a file or . . . soap?"

"What I got's *my* bidness," Beverly muttered. "Keep movin' while you got the chance."

That was the first skirmish. The war heated up from there.

Miss Landis wasn't great on grammar, though we did a lot of it. "Scooter Tomlinson," she sang out one day, "can you give me an example of an adverb?"

"Gladly," Scooter said.

But she didn't get it.

We put in hours up at the blackboard on grammar, four or five of us at a time, diagramming sentences. I never saw the reason behind this.

Scooter was diagramming next to me one time when he muttered, "Don't look now, but your participle's dangling." I looked down before I thought. Scooter was beginning to have a somewhat smart mouth, but we were older now.

When Miss Landis called Beverly to the board, Big Bev just pointed across the room and snapped her gnawed fingers at her stooge Doreen R. Doreen did Beverly's bidding and all her dirty work and heavy lifting.

"No, Doreen," Miss Landis said, flustered. "You, Beverly."

"I'm busy." Beverly lolled at her desk, snapping a rubber band. The classroom box of rubber bands had vanished from the teacher's desk, and they were the last for the duration.

Around this time, Miss Landis's purse disappeared. Janis W., Beverly's other full-time stooge, was wearing lipstick now, which wasn't allowed. Some of the girls said it was Miss Landis's shade. Jungle Dawn Pink, according to them.

In Miss Landis's missing purse was always a small blue bottle of Evening in Paris perfume, which she dotted on her wrists at recess. Doreen was wearing perfume, a load of it. She smelled like she'd dumped a full bottle of Evening in Paris over her head. It cut your eyes three rows away.

"P.U.," said a couple of girls too near Doreen. Later that same day they had bad falls in the school yard.

We waited for Miss Landis to take charge of the classroom, but she was pretty near tears most of the time. Then one fatal War Stamp Thursday came.

We brought our dimes and our stamp books up to the teacher's desk by rows. I had a dime extra reserved to pay off Doreen, who was collecting for Beverly that week. Then trouble broke out in Doreen's row.

Patty MacIntosh, a small, skinny girl, was pleading for her life. "But I only have a nickel left. I forgot." Doreen flipped the nickel in Patty's face. Then Doreen was out of her seat, and Patty's bird-brittle arm was being twisted behind her back, and she was shrieking. Miss Landis started. Pink stamps went all over.

"To the principal's office," Miss Landis said to Doreen, who'd turned Patty loose. This brought Beverly heaving out of her seat and snapping a finger at Janis. They all three stalked out the door.

"Not you, Beverly," Miss Landis said in a hopeless voice. "Not you, Janis . . ."

They didn't go to the principal's office either. But did we care? We last stamp buyers didn't have to pay the extra dime of protection money. Then just when the day was finally about over, we heard a siren.

Some people started to get under their desks. But the door banged back, and in strutted Beverly, Doreen, and Janis, looking really pleased with themselves. Beverly was as close to a grin as she ever got. Behind them came a cop, in uniform. G. K. Ingersoll, according to his badge. He was the real thing with a nightstick and a cartridge belt. It was kind of neat, and we stared.

Miss Landis hung at the front of the classroom, one hand slipping off the chalk tray.

"Miss," G. K. Ingersoll said, "are these yours?"

They'd been nabbed shoplifting at the Ben Franklin store. Sadly, the manager wasn't pressing charges. But Beverly and her stooges got most of a day off out of it and a ride in a police car, with siren.

The bell rang, and we went home. Beverly's bunch made a U-turn and left with us.

Miss Landis got through most of the next morning by not calling on any of the three of them. Then once again we got a visitor.

A giant figure appeared at the classroom door. We hadn't seen a woman this big since Mrs. Meece came for her girdle. She strode in, shoulders first, wearing overalls and a red bandanna wrapped around her head. And great big hobnail boots.

The war poster on the wall showed an assembly line of women riveters under a headline:

WE'RE THE JANES
WHO BUILD THE PLANES

This woman looked just like them, but more than life-size. We knew who she was. She was an even beefier Beverly. It was her mom. Had to be.

She scanned the rows for Beverly, who hardly flinched. Then Beverly's mom was at the front of the room with a finger in Miss Landis's face. "You. You the teacher?"

Miss Landis said she was, faintly.

"I'm on a cigarette break from the plant," Beverly's mom barked. "But the next time they nail her at Ben Franklin or wherever, I'll be docked a day's pay, bailing her out." She jerked a thumb back at Beverly, who was over the surprise of seeing her mom at school. She was close to a grin again.

Miss Landis whimpered.

"Do your job," Beverly's mom snapped. "I know she's no picnic, but KEEP THAT BRAT OFF THE STREETS WHILE I'M AT WORK."

You could have heard her all over the school. The principal did. As Beverly's mom barged out, Miss Howe was coming in. They jammed. Then Beverly's mom was gone, and Miss Howe was in the room, gazing across us at Miss Landis.

She'd slumped into her chair. Her head hung. We couldn't see her perfect hands, helpless in her lap.

She looked up at Miss Howe. "I can't do this," Miss Landis said.

We had a weekend to wonder.

"She'll be back," Scooter predicted. "It's nearly November. Where are they going to find anybody else? There's a war on."

But on Monday morning Miss Landis wasn't there. She hadn't even had to clean out her desk. Beverly and her stooges had done that for her weeks ago. We milled around and threw chalk until Miss Howe herself loomed into the room.

"People," she said, "Miss Landis has made the difficult decision to take up a position in war work, as so many teachers are doing these days."

Eyes rolled all over the room. Except for Walter Meece, just now noticing the teacher was absent.

"But we are fortunate in finding a replacement, whose patriotic duty is to step in on a moment's notice. I am sure you will all welcome her with your best behavior."

Beverly snorted.

Miss Howe looked at the door. We all did.

A figure stood in the door frame, dark against the glare of the hallway light.

It was like they'd turned Miss Landis inside out, and here was her opposite. Old and scary with eyes bugged by her spectacles and wearing a shapeless shroudlike garment. One withered fist was parked on her bony hip.

One of the girls screamed.

Scooter smacked his forehead.

I couldn't believe my eyes.

It was Miss Eulalia Titus.

In Scooter's Opinion . . .

. . . we'd gone out of the frying pan into the fire. Miss Landis had been too young to teach us. Miss Titus was too old to live.

It took us a while to adjust to her. We weren't used to a teacher who looked like a walnut with a mustache. With those specs, her eyes were bigger than she was, but you couldn't tell where she was looking. Maybe around corners.

The girls found out they missed Miss Landis. She'd worn a different outfit every day, and they'd drawn her dresses in their notebooks instead of learning. Miss Titus wore the same shroud every day. She wouldn't have had to paint her legs. They were nowhere in sight.

We supposed she'd be a bear on diagramming, but she said, "I gather you can all diagram sentences. Let's see if you can write one."

Composition? Hands smacked foreheads all over the room. Beverly stirred.

Beverly was biding her time. She'd run one teacher off, and this one looked like she already had one foot in the grave. "Lady," I personally heard Beverly mutter to herself, "I'll have you in the nursing home by Thanksgiving."

Our first composition was to be:

How We, the Young of America, Are Winning the War

While we wrote, I chanced a look Beverly's way. She was drawing a lopsided skull and crossbones across the page.

"Can we use the dictionary?" somebody asked.

"You better," Miss Titus said.

Wednesday was her day to supervise recess. We were to leave by rows, which was a new one on us. But even Beverly went quietly. Miss Titus left her pocketbook behind on the floor by her desk, sticking out. Great big cracked-leather handbag.

Hoyt Albers pointed it out. "Better not," he said, but Miss Titus didn't seem to hear.

After recess, she manned the outside door to see that we came back in one at a time. I remember Beverly brushing past her because they were the same height. Then we heard screaming from inside school, echoing down the halls. Big screams.

Teachers looked out of their classrooms. The screams came from ours.

Doreen was up by the teacher's desk, wringing her hands. Janis was on the floor at her feet, back arching, flailing around, howling. Something heavy was clamped to her hand, and she was banging it on the floor.

Another odd thing about Miss Titus, she could move like greased lightning. In a twinkling, she was at the front of the room, crouching over Janis. She grabbed her flopping hand and held it up.

We made a circle and gaped. All four of Janis's fingers were mashed into a big spring-action patented rattrap. It was a businesslike trap, though rusty. Her fingers sticking out were gray, and her nails were blue. Taking her time, Miss Titus sprung the trap open and took it off Janis. "Get my pocketbook," she told Doreen.

Janis was wracked with sobs, a weird sound coming from her. Jungle Dawn Pink lipstick was all over her face. She was one big smear, and her feet kicked. You'd hope there'd be some blood, but there wasn't. Still, her fingers were real flat.

Doreen collected Miss Titus's pocketbook from over in the corner where it had skidded. You could see how it happened. When Janis reached in to rifle the purse, the rattrap inside it got her. This was a surprise, and she jumped. The purse went flying.

"My stars," Miss Titus remarked. "I wonder how on earth a thing like that could have happened." She stood. "In your seats," she said, and we settled. Beverly too, looking around in her desk to make sure it hadn't been tampered with. The whole classroom could be a minefield.

Miss Titus told Patty MacIntosh to go with Janis to the girls' restroom to soak her fingers. We stirred.

Patty paled.

But her arm was in a sling, so she and Janis made a good match. One had a good arm, the other a good hand.

Beverly bolted. She and her stooges were never parted. It was a rule of theirs. She snapped a finger at Doreen, who was looking the other way. Then Beverly was lumbering up the aisle, heading for the door and Janis. Suddenly she was nose to nose with Miss Titus.

"What business is this of yours?" Two magnified eyes bored into Beverly.

Beverly fell back. A first. The tide of classroom war began to turn.

The whole business was a real good lesson about not stealing. And after she quit sobbing, what could Janis say? That a rattrap out of an old barn jumped up and bit her as she happened to be passing?

Some people thought baiting a rattrap with your purse wasn't the way a teacher should act. But nothing teacherish worked with Beverly or Doreen or Janis. Anyway, there was a war on, so you needed to bring out your big guns and your secret weapons.

When Patty MacIntosh and Janis came back, Miss Titus said to get ready for a lesson in first aid, as per the instructions on a wall chart. We were all in either Brownies or Cub Scouts by now, working on our bandaging badge, so we got busy on Janis, stretched out once more on the floor.

Her hand didn't look too bad, but she wouldn't be slapping anybody around with it for a while. Still, she hollered the place down every time you went near it. She was a lot bigger sissy than we'd realized.

With Miss Titus showing us how, we bandaged Janis up one side and down the other. She was a dead ringer for an Egyptian mummy by the time Miss Howe looked in on us, following Janis's screams. Miss Howe saw us at our patriotic best, working over Janis as volunteer victim, with actual tears.

"Very realistic," Miss Howe said, and withdrew.

War Stamp Thursday Came Around . . .

. . . and Miss Titus called out, "Scooter Tomlinson? How are you in arithmetic?" The wisp of scant hair atop her head seemed to form a question mark.

"A grade or two ahead," Scooter estimated.

So she put him and Hoyt Albers behind her desk, to take our money and issue the War Stamps, which they liked.

We were all used to returning to our desks by way of Doreen's row, to drop our dimes on her. But today Miss Titus was standing right over her. The first one down her aisle, Darryl Dillman, was ready with his dime. But there was Miss Titus, standing guard, all eyes. Doreen held her palm out, below the corner of her desk. But Miss Titus could see around corners.

"What's that dime for?" she demanded, loud enough for all.

"He . . . owes it to me," Doreen said in an all-new, mousy voice.

"What for?"

". . . For about a week," Doreen mumbled into her grubby shirtfront.

"Move on," Miss Titus told Darryl, and the line of dime-droppers behind him melted away.

"Nobody owes you a red cent, sister," Miss Titus said, over Doreen's head. But her buggish gaze swept the room and fell all over Beverly.

Beverly sizzled. An ugly flush rose up her brawny neck. She looked like she might burst into flames.

As one more of her stooges bit the dust. First Janis in the rattrap. Now Doreen without a dime.

Soon after, we got back our HOW WE, THE YOUNG OF AMERICA, ARE WINNING THE WAR essays. Scooter wrote about two boys who found a mutant form of milkweed growing in a barn, and they won the Congressional Medal of Honor for their discovery. Scooter liked using words such as *mutant*. Miss Titus wrote on his page that "It read well for fiction" and gave him a 94.

I wrote about a couple of boys who found a brass bed in a spooky attic and got a pair of movie tickets out of it. None of my participles dangled, but I'd written:

*"A lot of old stuff was laying around
the attic"*

when I should have written:

*"A lot of old stuff was lying around
the attic."*

She graded me down for that. Way down. Down, down, down. But it cured me.

Beverly got an F for her skull and crossbones, and stalked out of the room without her coat.

"Where's she going?" somebody said.

"Who?" Walter Meece said.

Where she went was Raycraft's Drug Store to order a cherry Coke she didn't pay for. She was nabbed going out the door with a bottle of eyedrops, a pair of dress shields, and a roll of Tums down her shirtfront, which must have been the first things she happened to see. All this came out later.

But Beverly sulked into school the next morning, and Miss Titus said nothing.

Then we got company again. They should have put a revolving door in for all the company we got. Beverly's mom was back, steaming like a kettle. The tails on her big bandanna vibrated, and she kicked the door on her way in. She was one burly woman.

We were doing fractions, and Miss Titus turned from the blackboard. Beverly's mom skidded to a stop. Nobody'd told her about Miss Titus, who would come as a surprise to anyone. For a moment, she might have thought this was Miss Landis after two months of us.

"Beverly's parent?" Miss Titus's eyebrows rose over her specs.

"Yes, and I'm on a cigarette break from the plant. What do you mean turning her loose to waltz out of sch—"

"I let her go," Miss Titus said.

"Why in th—"

"Because it was high time I saw you," Miss Titus said. "I can't picture you at a PTA meeting."

Beverly's mom simmered, but said, "Well, I can see you're no better than the last so-called teacher."

"Possibly worse," Miss Titus said. "They had to scrape the bottom of the barrel to find me. They had to burn the woods and sift the ashes. There's a war on, you know."

The nutcracker jaw on Beverly's mom clamped shut. Threats weren't going to work.

"You give her an F. It . . . upset her."

"An F's for not trying," Miss Titus said. "In this class you learn, or the police get involved. What's it going to be?"

That too slowed down Beverly's mom, way down. But she turned over a big hand. "Oh well, me and school never got along either."

"You mean school and I never got along either," Miss Titus said, correcting her. "Don't use bad English in front of my pupils. They need all the good examples they can get."

Beverly sat at her desk, kind of clenched up, just under their line of fire. We were all ears.

The sizzle went out of Beverly's big mom. Her voice fell a mile. "I make twice the wages here I made back home. But it ain't—isn't worth it."

She turned on Beverly, who was staring into the distance the way girls do around their mothers. "You're not cutting the mustard here," her mom told her. "They're going to have to win the war without me because I'm taking you back down home. I'll get my old job back, and when I'm not set—sitting on your head, your grandma will be."

Beverly erupted. "Grandma! NOT GRANDMA!"

We tried to picture her grandma, but couldn't.

Her mom checked the classroom clock and left.

It was nearly noon, but Miss Titus got us back to fractions in five-eighths of a second. When we left for lunch, Beverly stormed out first, opening the pocketknife she always carried to carve her desk with. We all gave her a running start. The other eight-to-five orphans opened their lunches. Doreen and Janis weren't sitting together.

When the coast was clear, Scooter and I strolled out to look along the curb for Miss Titus's banged-up Chevy with the suicide doors. When we spotted it, Scooter checked around on the street to find a pocketknife stuck in the flat front tire.

But it was worth it. Beverly was gone for good. And next semester Doreen made the honor roll. She was good at math, probably from counting all those dimes. And Janis did all right with her grades.

Over lunchtime I called Dad at the station to see if he could locate a tire for a '33 Chevy. He said he'd scout around and put out some feelers.

Without Beverly in school, it was like a day off.

In the afternoons, we had music, not Miss Titus's best subject. When she raised her voice in song, she sounded like her mama cawing from the bed. But we were warbling, "From the mountains to the prairies to the oceans white with foooaaam—" when we got our last visitor of the day.

It was Dad.

It was definitely Dad in the door, grinning and doffing his Phillips 66 cap. He and Miss Titus had about the same amount of hair. A recapped tire hung in his good arm. He spotted me, so he was in the right place. Then he saw Miss Titus.

And Miss Titus saw him. She lowered the pitch pipe and squinted through her specs. "Earl Bowman?"

I flinched.

"Yes, ma'am," Dad said, somewhat flushed. At home I'd never quite mentioned we didn't have Miss Landis anymore.

"That's my boy." Dad pointed me out.

"I knew he was yours as soon as I caught him in my barn," Miss Titus said.

I hadn't happened to mention that to Dad either.

"The apple never falls far from the tree," Miss Titus observed. "Remember the paddle?"

Dad winced and reached around behind himself.

"Teaching isn't what it was," Miss Titus remarked. "Why are you bringing a tire into my classroom?"

"You evidently need one, and we give full service," Dad said. "I have an idea your spare's shot."

"Tires are worth their weight in gold these days. There's a war on," Miss Titus said. "What are you charging for that tire? I see it's a Goodyear. And your labor, young man?"

Young man? The class gasped.

"Miss Titus, you don't owe me a thing," Dad said. "It's all the other way. You were the best teacher I ever had."

Miss Titus twitched. "I was the only teacher you ever had, Earl Bowman. All eight grades at Sangamon School."

"And the best," Dad said.

Under Miss Titus . . .

. . . we learned a lot more than we'd meant to. Spelling counted. Everything counted, and she ran our grade like Parris Island boot camp for the marines. She even brought Walter Meece almost up to speed.

Also Miss Titus was a St. Louis Cardinals fan, a big one. Months after the Dodgers threw away their lead, and the Cards went on to take the Series away from the Yankees, Miss Titus was using their stats in our arithmetic lessons.

I asked Dad if she'd had a mustache back when she taught him.

"It was just beginning," he said.

A classroom poster read:

USE IT UP, WEAR IT OUT
MAKE IT DO OR DO WITHOUT

To buy toothpaste now, you had to turn in the old used-up tube to the drugstore. Coffee vanished, and President Roosevelt told people to reuse their coffee grounds.

"I will if he will," Dad said.

Now the war effort needed kitchen fats and bacon grease. You were to save it up in a container. Then you got extra ration points when you took it to the grocer. Scooter said a single pound of cooking fat was glycerin enough for fifty .30-caliber bullets. A notice in the newspaper read:

LADIES: GET YOUR FAT CANS
DOWN TO THE STORE

which was the first time I'd heard Mom laugh in a while.

She was counting off the days till Christmas and having Bill home. He was night-flying now, and we were hoping he'd be done with that and home for the holidays.

But by December when the war was a year old, the army sent him straight on to bombardier school. The army seemed to change its mind a lot. He wrote from Deming, New Mexico, that they were training him on the Norden bomb sight. He had to strip and reassemble it in the dark, and they had to burn their class notes as soon as they'd memorized them.

So you had to be able to keep a secret.

Bill wouldn't be home, but Christmas crept up anyway. We pooled our sugar ration and baked early, to mail him his favorites.

"He'll be home in the spring before they ship them overseas. He'll be wearing his wings and his second lieutenant's bars, and he'll be on top of the world," Dad said, for Mom's benefit.

On Christmas Day we three went out hunting. Come to find out, Dad had taken Mom out hunting the day he asked her to marry him.

They carried their guns broken over their arms across the crusty fields. I walked in their frosty footprints. Dad's big treadmarks. The smaller prints of Mom's boots that laced up above her skirt tails. I walked behind them—Earl and Joyce Bowman. Pale sun played through the ice on the branches. They didn't kill anything, and I couldn't, not with a piddly Daisy air rifle, which wouldn't dent tin. But that wasn't why we were out here. If they'd seen anything to kill, they'd have let it go.

In the evening Mr. and Mrs. Smiley Hiser came over with a fruitcake from last year and their own ration of coffee. We sat in the safe kitchen with the steaming, streaming windows. We kept Christmas and waited for warm weather, and my brother Bill.

JALOPY JULY

Spring Took Its Sweet Time Coming . . .

. . . and Bill didn't get home till June.

They started rationing shoes that February, and my feet were growing faster than three pairs a year. We were down to twenty-eight ounces of meat a week and four ounces of cheese. Down in St. Louis they were eating horse meat.

On Tuesdays now we wore our Cub Scout uniforms to school, and the pack met afterwards. Scooter and I had been in and out of Cubs for a year. The pack kept collapsing under us. You needed a den mother, and you wanted it to be somebody else's mother, not yours. But our den mothers kept getting war jobs or moving away or just giving up.

Now Hoyt Albers's mom took us on. We did regulation army calisthenics in her front yard while she watched from the porch. Scooter and I thought we were getting a little old for this. Knowing the secret Cub handshake and what WEBELOS meant wasn't the big deal it used to be. But we thought we had a great Cubmaster. This was a Boy Scout who came to our meetings and took charge of our pack.

Ours was Carlisle Snyder, who wore his Scout uniform plastered with badges and medals to our den meetings. We tied a lot of knots under his direction, and he was pretty good with Walter Meece, who needed extra time for everything. Carlisle was in ninth grade, taller than Mrs. Albers, and shaved. He was pretty much who all us Cubs wanted to be.

Besides, the Community Paper Drive was starting up, the biggest collecting campaign of the war so far, and we were competing citywide as Cub dens and Scout troops.

Scooter wasn't crazy about wearing his Cub blue and yellow, even the neckerchief. "There's more to war than wearing a uniform," he said. But we wore ours when we paired up for the paper drive.

Off we went again, pulling our wagons over the old scrap metal route. More people worked now and weren't home during the day. We were back in the Country of the Old. Not Mr. Stonecypher. There wasn't any paper in his attic, and his basement was off-limits because of the still.

"Old Lady Graves?" Scooter said.

"You knock," I said.

"What this time?" she said when she flung open her back door. She was about Miss Titus's age, but not as good-looking. Her scalp bristled with curlers. She had enough metal on her head to build a Jeep.

"Paper," Scooter said. "When we turn in a thousand pounds apiece, we get General Eisenhower's medal."

"Do tell," she said. "Start with the basement."

It was real dank, though she'd kept every paper ever delivered to her. But water stood in her basement, and the newspapers had mostly turned into towers of foul mush. We took from the top and were up and down her back stairs with yellow piles.

Then she sent us up to her attic. "While you're up there, bring down my dress dummy."

We moaned.

"And my sewing machine. I've got to start making my own clothes again," Old Lady Graves hollered. "There's a war on, you know."

Her dress dummy looked like her, but better. It had no head. Her sewing machine was a foot-pedal Singer with a rubber drive belt. It would be swell scrap, and it outweighed us. It barely budged, but we got it down, a stair step at a time. Only then could we go back for her collection of *Saturday Evening Post*s and *Ladies' Home Journal*s.

Hefting a stack higher than his head, Scooter tripped over something and fell flat. Magazines flew. I didn't laugh, but it was funny, and he'd skinned his knee. He'd tripped over a bag of something. "What is it anyway?" he said.

It was a hundred pounds of sugar.

"Old Lady Graves is a hoarder," Scooter whispered, which was no big surprise. We looked closer at the dusty bag. It was hard as a rock, and moth- and mouse-eaten. The lettering on it was faded. Scooter smacked his forehead. It was from World War I.

We sat on it, wringing wet from all our work. Scooter still thought we were giving too much to the war effort. But we wanted those medals of General Eisenhower's.

We were even-steven about it, piling half our paper on Scooter's back porch, half on mine. We'd finally figured out we had to take twine and tie our scrap paper into bundles. We were dragging full loads home one afternoon when a big stake-bed REO truck pulled up beside us. Three Boy Scouts from Troop 15 were up in the cab. The one at the wheel was an Eagle Scout, old enough to drive. He had badges all over him.

We were pulling these puny Radio Flyer wagons that kept tipping over, and now we looked up. It was a marvel how much paper you could get with a truck and a whole troop collecting together. Six or eight Scouts stood up there in the truck bed in the paper piles. The Eagle Scout leaned out from the driver's seat.

"You two. We'll take your paper."

We tried not to get any smaller when the Scouts jumped down off the truck.

"It's ours," Scooter said. "We collected it." But his voice hadn't changed yet.

"You want to fight eleven of us for it, squirt?" the Eagle Scout said. "Put up your dukes." And they all snorted. Scout snorts.

They were already heaving our bundles up into the truck. They'd been heavy to us, but nothing to the Scouts. And what could we do? It was Troop 15 too, Carlisle Snyder's troop.

If he was here, he wouldn't let them pull this on us, I thought.

I looked up, and he was right there, in uniform, our paper in his arms. One of the gang.

Scooter saw. Who could miss our so-called Cubmaster? We stared, which is all we could do. But he never looked us in the eye. After they'd gunned off, we still watched all the way to the corner, but he wouldn't look back.

We were both about to cry, but not over the paper. Scooter unknotted his Cub neckerchief. He went up to a Dutch elm growing next to the Friedingers' curb and tied the neckerchief to the highest limb he could reach. It had something to do with not being a Cub if it led to being a Scout. Anyway, we didn't mess much with Cubs after that, but I know for a fact that Carlisle Snyder never came to another den meeting.

We got our General Eisenhower medals. The paper wasn't the problem. When they weighed ours, we were way over, but I never wore the medal. I figured Carlisle Snyder was wearing his.

Scooter and I went on home that afternoon. Our empty wagons rattled, and we were back in time for *The Lone Ranger* on the radio. So that part was the same. But *we* were different.

By That Summer of 1943 . . .

. . . the town was pretty well picked clean. Now even copper pennies had rolled off to war. The 1943 pennies were steel and zinc. A lot of them passed for dimes before people got wise to them.

Scooter and I had done our share for the effort. Even the idea of Old Lady Graves's sewing machine gnawed at us, though we never got it. But we didn't go near paper again, never mentioned it.

Now the Chamber of Commerce announced a Jalopy Parade as the main event of the summer, to shake loose still more scrap metal. There were old hulks of cars around that needed to go to war because they weren't going anywhere else.

The plan snowballed. Now they were talking about crowning a Jalopy Queen for a procession of decorated clunkers and high school bands. It was going to wind through downtown and end at Sol Tick's scrap yard.

In the middle of parade mania, Bill came home. He didn't call from the Wabash depot, and we didn't hear the taxicab. We were just sitting down to supper at the kitchen table. I can still see the light of that summer evening slanting in the window. Bill walked in, wearing his second lieutenant's uniform and his bars. And his wings. Silver wings. It was Bill, leaner, with Dad's grin. He whipped off his cap, and it rolled on the linoleum.

I remember Mom's hands flying to her face and the kitchen swimming. I remember Dad coming out of his chair that fell over behind him.

In a crate out by the garage Dad had been feeding up two chickens for this moment. I was out there when he wrung the neck off first one, then the other. His good hand was a windmill, and the birds pinwheeled in the air, feathers white on the grass like summer snow. In the long evening shadows Dad did kind of a dance between the flopping fowls.

The Hisers were out, working their victory garden. When they saw Dad dancing in that fall of floating feathers, they knew Bill was home. They capered down their runner-bean row, cackling.

Dad and I plucked the chickens over buckets of boiling water down in the basement, letting Mom have Bill to herself. We cleaned and dressed the birds and soaked them in cold pink salt water.

Upstairs they popped in the pan, and the potatoes were on the boil. Then Dad was laying into them with the masher and all our butter, and Mom was going for the company dishes.

The Hisers brought over the last of their strawberries and shortcake to go with them. But they wouldn't stay. They were in and out because every minute mattered, with Bill here.

He'd brought presents. Beaded moccasins for Mom, a hunting knife in a tooled Mexican leather sheath for Dad. My present was upstairs.

It wasn't quite dark. This was the longest day of the year. I watched Bill pull his kit out of his musette bag and lay it out on the bed like an inspection. The dress shoes like patent leather, those Brassoed buttons, the wings. There was a pair of fleece-lined boots and a cap and big, fleecy gloves. The bed was woolly as a sheep. But there by the pillow was the pen wiper I'd made in Miss Mossman's class.

"You know what these mean?" Bill held up the thick gloves. He looked down at me, but not as far down as before.

"It's cold up there?" I said. "That high up?"

"And down below too."

So I almost knew he wasn't heading anywhere hot, like the South Pacific or Africa. It was almost a secret, and I thought I could keep it.

I was following Bill's every move when he pulled the red and white letter sweater out of the closet. "You're ready for this, aren't you?"

I was starting to shoot up, so yes. He gave me the sweater on the first night, not his last. He didn't make me wait.

I told him about the Jalopy Parade. The sponsored jalopies, the decorations, the floats, the marching bands, the Parade Queen. Flags waved all over our particular world, but it must be small-time stuff, piddly, if you wore wings and could strip a bomb sight in the dark.

"Where's ours?" Bill asked.

"Our what?"

"Our jalopy. Representing the Earl Bowman and Sons Phillips 66 Gas and Oil Station?"

But it didn't work that way. Sponsors were bigger outfits, lots bigger: Block & Kuhl's department store and the American Legion and the starch works and the League of Women Voters.

The attic was all shadow now. Bill switched on a light. Another one went on in my head.

"There's one in Miss Titus's barn," I said, "if she'd let us have it, which she wouldn't in one million years."

But She Would . . .

. . . Miss Titus would let us have her ancient auto, let us parade it with the jalopies, send it off for scrap. When we went out to see her, Bill wore his uniform, and maybe that clenched the deal.

We drove out after Dad closed up the station, out Wyckles Corner way in the growling Packard, three across. The family car was a '36 Pontiac sedan that Mom drove. But you'd need the Packard to get up Miss Titus's lane. It was one rock after another.

Though it was evening, she was on her porch, and it was like the first time, but without the shotgun. She leaned on a hoe for the snakes.

Summer had come, and she wasn't my teacher anymore, and I never learned as much from another one. When we were in the weeds of her yard, her voice rang out, "Earl Bowman? Talk about a bad penny."

But even then Bill in his uniform filled her specs. She lit a lantern and led us down to the webby barn. Over her feed-sack dress she wore a carpenter's apron. Its pockets brimmed with stuff: a ball-peen hammer, a paperback Webster's dictionary, a box of kitchen matches. She held the lantern up to the auto.

"By golly, it's a Pan American," Dad said. "The only automobile ever built in this town."

"My father bought this one at the factory door," she said. "One of the first. He gave six hundred and fifty dollars for it. Cash, naturally."

"They weren't in business long. This is just about one-of-a-kind." Dad had to get closer, under the missing hood.

"Miss Titus, maybe it ought to be restored," Bill said, "in a museum."

She turned on him, though the lantern never bobbled. "Where are you going next in that uniform, young man?"

"I'm not supposed to say, ma'am."

She saw the Eighth Air Force insignia.

"England," she said, "for raids over Hamburg, Cologne, Berlin, the Ruhr valley. The submarine pens off the coast of France?"

"If you say so, ma'am."

"B-17s?" she said. "Flying Fortresses?"

Now Dad was listening, from the auto.

"How many missions will you fly?" Miss Titus asked.

"Twenty-five, ma'am."

A moment in the dark barn lingered. You could hear a rumble in the evening sky. Then Miss Titus said, "When you've flown your last mission and are back home with us, then it'll be time to talk about restoring things and putting them in museums."

The Jalopy Parade . . .

. . . our own Rose Bowl of Wrecks, was the biggest blowout in the summer of '43. That was the middle summer of the war, though we didn't know it. We only knew it was time to cut loose.

On the hottest day, here came G. K. Ingersoll in a Plymouth police car, not scrap, blaring his sirens to clear the parade route. The high school band stepped out behind him with "Coming in on a Wing and a Prayer," in march time. The majorettes of the Red Pepper pep squad flung their glitter batons as high as five-story buildings.

The mayor rode in an open Pierce-Arrow four-door, missing three doors and the radiator. It was towed by a team from the Meadow Gold Dairy. Milk was delivered by horse-drawn wagons, and every dairy horse in town was pulling a jalopy.

Two big Percherons from the brewery pulled the Emerson Piano House's 1937 woody Ford station wagon that had suffered a bad fire. The Daughters of the American Revolution rode on rims in a peeled-roof Studebaker Dictator that had flipped several times. They were pulled by a road grader decked with Revolutionary War flags, proclaiming:

DON'T TREAD ON ME

and

LIVE FREE OR DIE

Then here came the Taylorville High School band belting out "We Did It Before and We Can Do It Again."

Van Natta's Funeral Home was donating an old Chrysler hearse of theirs that still ran, barely. The windows were out, and against a wreath of weeds on the coffin was a sign reading:

HERE LIES MUSSOLINI
PLENTY OF ROOM INSIDE
FOR TWO MORE

—meaning Hitler and Hirohito.

And for as far as you could see, flags and more flags, and some jitterbugging in the streets between bands.

Three high school senior guys, graduated now, were donating their Model A ragtops, though they still ran. If you were a high school hotshot, you drove an old Ford Model A to school and cruised around and around the building at lunchtime.

Now they were turning in their Fords before reporting to basic training. The rumbleseats were full of girls, and the latest song titles were scrawled all over the hoods and doors:

PRAISE THE LORD AND
PASS THE AMMUNITION

and

THE BOOGIE-WOOGIE
BUGLE BOY OF COMPANY B

and

SO LONG, MAMA,
I'M OFF TO YOKOHAMA

There were thirty-eight jalopies in all, which Scooter calculated would add up to a landing craft.

The entry fee was a fifty-dollar war bond. Somehow, Dad pulled the money out of thin air. Working into the nights, he and Bill had unfrozen the axles on the Pan American and found four tired tires, bald as Miss Titus's mama and of various sizes.

Once we got the auto hosed down, it had a real good coat of deep red lacquer paint on it, which we buffed. Scooter and I went to work with a can of Brasso on the brightwork. We painted whitewalls on the tires. Mom resewed the upholstery, and we laid plywood where the floors were missing.

A lot of jalopies were painted all over: song titles and sayings like "Don't Make a Yankee Cranky." Some of them were too rusted out to say anything. But our polished jalopy was going to go out in style with everything but a hood and a horn.

We thought we'd tow it, but Dad said they might want the Packard too. He didn't see why we couldn't rig up some kind of engine to get us as far as the scrap yard. He had a little Willys-Knight motor he tinkered with. Its transmission was near death, and it had no reverse gear. But he and Bill got it slung in the car and introduced it to the driveshaft. A lot of baling wire was involved.

And now we were in the staging area, behind the high school Model A's, waiting our turn in the parade. Dad was behind the wheel, wearing his Shriner's fez. Scooter and I were up there with him. Mom sat on the backseat with Bill in his uniform.

Behind us, a team of plumed white dairy horses pawed the pavement, ready to go. They were hitched up to a float, which was the centerpiece of the parade. It was a Wizard of Oz castle with tin can towers, blinding in the sun. On top was the Jalopy Queen and her court. She sat in a throne made out of chrome car bumpers with her court arranged around her in their prom dresses, carrying tinfoil bouquets.

Bill looked back. "That's not—"

"Diana Powers," Mom said.

She'd have been a few years behind Bill in school. And of course he'd never seen her wearing a crown of gilded sink-stoppers on top of a parade float. And a real low-cut prom dress. She was the best-looking girl in the county, by far. Even I noticed, and I was just beginning to notice these things. Her family lived on top of Moreland Heights and owned all the grain elevators between here and Pana. Diana Powers looked down from on high.

"Bill?" she called out. "Bill Bowman?"

He stood. The Pan American swayed. His wings winked as he turned.

"Bill Bowman," she called down. "I've always had such a crush on you. Get up here."

Our turn came. The Willys-Knight motor labored, and we made the corner into Water Street past the Hotel Orlando, the Busy Bee Shoeshine Parlor. The Model A ragtops were getting a roar from the crowd. But ours was the best jalopy, and the sign on the re-hung door read:

THE PAN AMERICAN
hometown made
and ready to rain
on Hitler's parade

Scooter wrote it.

Behind us came the Jalopy Queen's float. High in the air like the figures on a wedding cake were Diana Powers, nodding to the crowd, and standing above her my brother Bill, and both of them golden in the rust, white, and blue day.

THE STAR IN THE
WINDOW

Four Stars Hung on Our Street . . .

. . . blue stars on little white flags in front windows. Ours for Bill and the Runions' for Cleve, the Rogerses' for Jinx, the Tomlinsons' for Scooter's dad. They were the landmarks now that nobody played much hide-and-seek around the Hisers' box elder tree.

We followed Bill as far as we could, in our minds and the mail. He met up with his ten-man crew in Oklahoma for eight weeks of training on the B-17 Flying Fortress, shortened to six.

Scooter and I had plane-spotting books. We never spotted anything but a Piper Comanche, but we knew the particulars of a B-17: the 104-foot wingspan, the four motors, the tail gunner folded into the Plexiglas dome, covering them from behind with two .50-caliber guns.

They named their plane the *Baby Snooks* after a little girl on the radio played by a grown-up lady. Heading east, they flew somewhere over us, getting the hang of it. Bill wrote from Gander, Newfoundland.

In another night after that, they flew across the Atlantic. Their flight suits were wired for warmth.

When Bill wrote from Somewhere in England, the letters were V-mail—flimsy blue sheets. His crew was flying missions over the enemy now. When the bomb bay doors opened, I wondered if you could see the bombs all the way down to the ground, like in the newsreels. The Americans flew the day raids. The British flew the night ones.

In the evenings Dad lay on the living room floor in front of the Philco with his head propped in the crook of his good arm. We listened to Richard Hottelet broadcasting from London, telling about crews parachuting out of burning bombers, hanging in the air with the sky on fire.

Dad listened, and Mom watched him listening. In October our B-17s were bombing Schweinfurt, trying to knock out the ball bearing factories. Now we were losing more planes than came back.

When Dad realized they were sending out those big B-17s like Bill's without any fighter planes to cover for them, something coiled tight inside him.

There were long strings of empty days without letters. Then Bill wrote three pages about how they'd had to ditch in the English Channel. The German fighters had raked them with gunfire from nose to tail. One engine caught fire, and they had to dive for enough air speed to put out the flames. A 20-millimeter shell cut the fuel line. They were coming in on a wing and a prayer, and they didn't make it back to home base.

I pictured Bill running and jumping hedges, trying to tag out on the Hisers' box elder, and never quite making it.

They were in the water till morning in the one raft that inflated, praying to be picked up by our side. They wore their Mae Wests, their life jackets, and I wondered whose milkweed was stuffed inside. Not all of them got back, but Bill did. Then come to find out, that flight didn't even count as one of Bill's twenty-five missions because they didn't complete it.

There were things he couldn't put in a letter. But we knew the *Baby Snooks* was at the bottom of the choppy English Channel. Bill said your first plane was like your first love. He never mentioned the name of any of the other planes he flew, not even the last one.

What the Government Wanted Now . . .

. . . was spider's thread wound onto reels to make the cross-hairs for gunsights and bomb sights. Now they were drafting spiders. But these threads weren't anything you could collect, for all the webby attics Scooter and I had pilfered through. It was a job for experts.

Besides, what Scooter? He was gone, since the second week of school. When the navy decided his dad was too old to ship overseas, they gave Mr. Tomlinson a desk job on North Island in San Diego.

The Tomlinsons rented out their house to war workers, four to a room. Scooter and his mom and the Schwinn took the Super Chief train to California. He sent one postcard from Coronado Island, and that was the last of Scooter for the duration. There I was, high and dry, with junior high still most of a year away.

I was moping home from school one afternoon, from Mrs. Spicer's class this year. It was early in November, because the leaves were coming down. There was the Cub Scout neckerchief Scooter had tied in the Friedingers' Dutch elm. It was faded and wind-whipped, but you could still see the Cub yellow and blue. It took me back.

A top-heavy old black car gunned past me up the empty street, a 1931 Buick, in fact. Luggage-rack back and taillights up on stalks. The license plate hanging by a screw. It was all over the street, weaving from curb to curb, scattering leaves. So I had to know, even before it took a wide swing up into our driveway.

It could only be Grandma and Grandpa Riddle, with Grandpa fighting the wheel. I lit out, and the Buick was by our back porch door.

Grandma Riddle began to spill out of the car. I hadn't seen her since before the war, and she was even bigger. The doorpost knocked her hat sideways, and her furpiece had a face with ears and eyes.

"Say listen, young man," she hollered at me, "go in that house and find my grandson Davy. He's a weedy little twerp. In fact, he's small potatoes and few in the hill. About knee-high to a grasshopper."

"I'm Davy, Grandma."

She fell back across the front seat and swatted Grandpa with her pocketbook. "Elmore! Fire this thing up and take me back home. This overgrown galoot is trying to pass hisself off as my grandson."

"I am your grandson, Grandma."

Her gaze glittered through trifocals. She'd known all along. She planted a huge lace-up shoe on the driveway. "Elmore," she said over her shoulder. "Give me a shove. We're staying."

Then Mom was there at the back porch door. Very pale. Pale as Patty MacIntosh.

"Mama," she murmured. ". . . For one thing, where did you get the gas to come all the way here?"

"Drained it out of the tractor," Grandma said. She was fighting her way out of the Buick. I wanted to help, but I didn't know what to reach for. Her furpiece was strangling her. The little fox face was snapping at her ear. Grandpa Riddle was climbing out on his side, slow, unlocking his knees.

"Papa," Mom said, softer.

"We'd have written ahead, honey," he said over the car, "but we thought you'd turn us back."

He came around the car. Talk about weedy. When he took my hand, his was like cornshucks. He was too wrinkled to shave.

He didn't kiss Mom, but he put an old stained finger under her chin and looked at her over his specs.

"Davy," Grandma said, "gather up all my reticules and valises off the backseat." Grandma had brought everything she owned. The floor was crammed with Ball jars of home canning. Pickled peaches and watermelon pickle and pig's feet and rhubarb.

Grandma was on her feet now, weaving, looking for her land legs. They'd been all over both lanes of the hard road for hours, from below DuQuoin. She looked Mom up and down.

"Joyce, you look like a gully beginning to wash. What you could use is a dose of salts and a square meal."

We were all four by the back door. Grandma jerked her big coat around her. "My stars and garters, it's cold up here. I don't know how you'ens live in it."

Mom bit her lip. Her lips were thin today, though usually she was pretty. She and Grandma never had hit it off. The war had been a good excuse for not visiting, till now.

"We had to come," Grandma thundered. "It was a matter of life and death. Two poor old parties like us can't get by on that sugar ration. I don't mind honey in my coffee, when we can get coffee. But Elmore won't have it."

She pointed down at Grandpa. He was half the size of Mr. Hiser, and she was three Mrs. Hisers.

"And what about gasoline for country people?" Grandma wanted to know. "I can't get in to the store, and we've been riding on fumes since Blue Mound. And the back tires are from off the tractor."

Grandpa looked down the Buick at a back tire. It was caked with mud from the field. Using tractor tires on a public road was against the law.

"We're going to have to gang in here with you'ens in your front bedroom for the time being," Grandma said. "That's all there is to it. There's a war on, you know. And where's Earl Bowman? Working, I hope to heaven. Joyce, you remember what I said before you married him." She waved Mom aside. "And get out of the door. I'm coming in."

Mom's hands worked in her apron. Her knuckles were whiter than her face.

All Europe Waited for the Invasion . . .

. . . that didn't come till D-day in the next year. But we got *our* invasion early. Grandma and Grandpa Riddle settled into the spare room downstairs, and we were a full house. They brought their ration books, so there were more red points for meat and cheese, and sugar for baking.

But five of us were using the bathroom now. And Grandma Riddle was everywhere you turned and bigger than some of our rooms.

Mom had always been in charge of the house and Dad and me, and she did a really good job. She was the top mom of the world, it seemed to me. But overnight she turned into a daughter, and Grandma ruled.

As she often said, "Idle hands are the devil's workshop," so when she wasn't showing Mom how to clean house or cook, she was crocheting terrible doilies for the davenport and antimacassars for the chairs.

Mom drew the line at going to the grocery store with Grandma. I had to walk her there, and it wasn't a good experience. She wanted to go every day, and the grocer didn't like her. She squeezed the fruit. And she'd say things like, "Give me a ten-pound sack of weevils and throw in some flour." Which he also didn't like.

Mom fell back on every front, but hung on, living for the mail delivery. When a long time went by without word from Bill, Grandma would say, "No news is good news." Which also grated on Mom.

Dad and Grandpa Riddle did a lot better. Most mornings Grandpa climbed into his bib overalls and went off to work with Dad in the Packard. He was pretty good help at the station. The pumps were electric now, so he never quite got the hang of pumping gas. But being a farmer, he could repair anything. Mostly he hung out on the pump island with the other codgers, and they showed him respect because he was Earl Bowman's father-in-law.

We made it to Thanksgiving, and an eighteen-pound turkey appeared from somewhere. All the fixings were like before the war, and the Hisers came. Mrs. Hiser said Grandma Riddle's cornbread stuffing was the best thing she ever put in her mouth. Grandma said she'd show Mom how to make it.

So it was a long day, and at the end Mom took Dad down to the basement and told him she couldn't take another minute of it. She was going to have to go out and get a job. She was either going to have to get out of the house or go out of her mind.

On Monday she was working in the office at the blood bank. By Christmastime she was running it. That suited Grandma fine. She said she could finally give our house the cleaning it needed. "The dust around here is thicker than the fur on a squirrel." She promised that when a letter came from Bill, she'd call Mom at the blood bank as quick as she'd read it.

Droning Bombers Fanned Out Over Europe . . .

. . . and fleets of big black Lincolns fanned out from Chicago. Lincoln Continentals mostly, and some of them headed down our way. The Chicago mob was selling counterfeit gas coupons to filling station operators.

Gas rationing worked like this. If you had a ration book of "A" coupons, you got three gallons of gas a week. Period. If you had a "B" coupon book, you were a war worker or a traveling salesman and got a little more. But a "C" coupon was the Big Time. That meant you were a doctor or a cop, and you got a lot more. When Dad learned that Congress in

Washington voted themselves "X" coupon books, meaning all the gas they wanted, something coiled in him again.

Now the Chicago mobs were working our territory, big black beetles swarming over our world. They were selling counterfeit "C" coupons to gas stations. The stations could sell gas twenty cents a gallon over the ceiling, then cover up the illegal sales by turning in the counterfeit coupons to the OPA.

They said that thirty-five percent of all the gas sold up in Chicago was with bogus coupons. Fifty percent in New York. It was a sweet deal. But when the big bozos in snap-brim hats came to Dad with a deal he couldn't refuse, he threw them out. They said they'd be back, with a fifty-dollar starter set of "C" coupons, and they'd expect it in cash.

They came back in a Lincoln one December day, waiting until Dad and Grandpa were between customers. All of a sudden they were swarming around the place, big guys in pinky rings. They told Dad to dip fifty dollars out of the safe. He said he'd call the cops, and the mobsters laughed. They showed him the coupon book he was supposed to buy from them, and he told them where to put it.

So one of them came up behind Dad and swung a monkey wrench against the side of his head. His cap flew off, and his glasses. He fell sideways on the pavement on his bad arm, and didn't move. They did this to my dad.

Then they stuck the bloody wrench under Grandpa's chin and said they'd make an example out of him too. He was eighty-three years old, and he just looked at them. They piled into the Lincoln and left.

It was a school day, so I didn't know till I got home. Grandma was holding the fort. Mom had gone straight to the hospital. Grandpa Riddle was running the station, but Grandma wanted him home.

We went in shifts to the hospital, and the Hisers were there every day. On the second night I was there with Grandpa. Dad looked smaller in the bed, smaller than he could make himself on Halloween night. In the hospital nightshirt, he wasn't himself. There were stitches in the side of his head, and the concussion made him see two of everything. He looked wrung out—like a gully beginning to wash. And the hospital food was like the army's.

We were down to the end of the visiting hours. The nurses' aids were piling the bedpans. Standing up, Grandpa wasn't a lot taller than Dad's bed. He had worked a full day, keeping the station going.

"I don't know what I'd do without you, Mr. Riddle," Dad said. He always called Grandpa Mr. Riddle.

"Pshaw," Grandpa said. "We pitch in. It's how we do it down home in the southern part of the state, Earl."

I watched them in the shadowy room. My dad. My grandpa.

"Of course, running your place of business wasn't what we come up here for," Grandpa remarked. "Nor takin' on all them Chicago Al Capones."

"I wondered." Dad spoke from deep in the pillow. "It would take something to get you two off the farm and out of Williamson County. It wasn't the sugar, was it? Or the gas."

Grandpa shook his old smooth head. "No. We were gettin' along. If there's anything we know, it's how to do without."

A little quiet fell. Then Grandpa said, "It was the radio. We tune in a good deal. We heard about the raids the boys are flying over Germany and them places. We heard about the toll the Nazi fighters and the flak was taking on boys like Bill. Finally, the wife said she had to be up here with her daughter. She needed to be here for Joyce."

"Ah," Dad said.

"So up we come," Grandpa said, "to get Joyce out of the house and into a job somewheres. The wife says that waitin' on the mail is an old woman's job."

My head swam. Grandma *planned* to run Mom out of the house? For her own good? She wanted Mom to get a job so she wouldn't just be home, waiting? My head throbbed.

"She means well, you know," Grandpa said. "The wife."

"I know now," Dad said.

Grandpa and I drove home in the Buick. He was a scarier driver after dark. Things kept looming up, and he held the steering wheel like reins.

"Grandpa," I said, "do you have a license?"

"Of course I've got a license." He ground a gear. "How else could I hunt?"

"I mean a driver's license, Grandpa."

"A what?" he said, jumping the curb as he turned into our street too soon.

When the Telegram Came . . .

. . . Grandma was there to sign for it. She called Dad from the station and Mom from the blood bank, and she didn't open it. I came in from school, and there they were, the three of them with the yellow envelope in Dad's hand. Grandma Riddle hovered behind Mom.

We'd made it through Christmas, and a letter from Bill came like a present. It was January now, of 1944, and Bill was missing in action.

It was on that giant raid over Stuttgart—three hundred and thirty aircraft. But everything went wrong. Cloud cover scattered the bomber force, and half of them had to look for other targets. The Luftwaffe fighters were all over them with head-on attacks. Forty-five bombers were lost. Bill's plane was.

The telegram didn't tell us that much. It only said he was missing. But we were wise to the war now, from Bill's letters and the radio. We knew all the things that *missing* could mean. If they parachuted out of the plane over Germany and nobody shot them coming down or killed them when they landed—if they were prisoners of war, we'd get a postcard about that. From the Red Cross in Switzerland, sooner or later.

And if he came down alive in France, it depended on who found him.

And if they crash-landed the plane in the English Channel, that too depended on who found them. But it was a January heaving with ice, so they wouldn't last long in the water. The wires in their flight suits wouldn't be working. The milkweed wouldn't matter.

It Was the Worst Time . . .

. . . that winter when we walked through the days.

Just because Mom never missed work at the blood bank didn't meant I was an eight-to-five orphan. I came home every noon, my feet crowding my shoes because the rations book said I wasn't due a new pair till March.

Now in frozen January, Grandma Riddle fixed me my lunch, hot biscuits and gravy, a caldron of simmering soup, thick enough for a mouse to walk across. She had less to say than before. We listened to her soap opera on the kitchen radio, *Lorenzo Jones and His Wife, Belle*.

Dad was working the pumps in his fleece jacket with Grandpa helping, business as usual. Dad's stitches were out, and his vision was back. The cops hadn't been as interested in the attack on him as you'd think. It was in the paper, though:

LOCAL STATION OWNER
ATTACKED BY OUT-OF-TOWNERS

Mrs. Hiser pasted the clipping into her scrapbook of car wrecks and house fires.

It was almost real life we were living, but not really. It was just waiting, and I didn't know if I was a brother or not.

I got up in the middle of the night one time. I don't know why. I didn't have to go that bad. The floor numbed my feet as I padded down to the bathroom. The whole world seemed asleep, so I jumped back when the bathroom light hit me.

What if it's Grandma in there? I backpedaled in panic. But it was Dad sitting on the rim of the bathtub, holding a hot towel to his bad arm and his aching shoulder. It was like my first memories of him. He'd always been up a lot at night with his arm.

He was only wearing pajama pants, and his feet were white on the white tile. He didn't hear me coming, or something. He jumped, and the hot towel came away from his shoulder. His eyes widened behind the glasses.

"I thought you were Bill," he said.

I stood there. How could he?

"Look at your feet," he said. "You'll be wearing my shoes." He had a good pair of Florsheims for church and the lodge. And he thought I was Bill?

"You're going to be taller than he is."

Is, not was. Is. Is. And all I wanted to ask Dad was: Will he come back? Because when you're a kid, your dad knows everything and can hear a Halloweener a mile off, behind a building. Except I wasn't a kid, quite.

Now I'd forgotten why I'd come down here. Dad fished the hot towel out of the tub.

"Dad, how did that happen?" I pointed at his bad arm and the shoulder the army'd had to put back together. It was red and rippled from the hot towel. I broke the rule because you weren't supposed to mention his war.

"When I made sergeant, I was a courier," he said. "I carried messages back and forth from the front. In France. The roads were blacked out and bad. I drove my motorcycle into a bomb crater. Tore my shoulder loose, bunged up my arm. Saved my life."

I looked up.

"They sent me home, and I lived. I was in the Veterans' Hospital till right into 1919. Then I had to kick the morphine they'd given me for the pain. So that was my war."

And more than I'd ever heard. "Did you hate it?"

"Every minute. And it wasn't the mud or the cold or even the eats."

I waited.

"It was what people do to each other."

I was trying to put it together in my mind. "So when Bill went, to this war . . ."

"I thought my war meant he wouldn't have to fight. I thought I'd failed him. I thought I'd let him down."

Then the terrible thing happened. Tears started out of Dad's eyes and ran down under his glasses. My dad was crying, and this was why you shouldn't talk about his war. I didn't know what to do.

My feet moved me forward, and I was right there in front of him. Still his tears came, and he looked away. I saw where they'd snipped out the stitches in his face. And he was still crying, quiet in the night.

I leaned over a little, being that tall now. "Be Dad," I said. "Be Dad."

He straightened up, whipped off his glasses, swiped his eyes with the back of his hand.

"That I will always be," he said, and the words rang off the tiles.

"But I can't be Bill," I said. Almost a wail.

He grabbed my shoulders. "You don't have to be. We'll get Bill back."

Grandma Stood Guard . . .

. . . through the winter weeks. When I'd come home for noon, she'd be in the front window, filling it up, because a telegram could come at any time of the day. And the star she stood behind was silver now because someone of ours was missing in action.

Grandpa missed open country. The next best thing was the park that started where our street ended. Scooter and I had roamed all over it when we were kids. It was acres of sledding hills, a pond, picnic tables. At the other end was a forest preserve with trails blazed by the WPA.

Grandpa liked tramping out there in his big old snub-nosed hightopper shoes. We'd head out on a Sunday afternoon, and one time we came across a stand of sassafras trees, brittle in the wind.

He always had his folding knife on him, and he fell to work, digging the roots and bark. Over time, we brought back bushels of the stuff, though you weren't supposed to dig anything up. But Grandpa didn't quite get the idea of what a park is. "Country's country," he said, and went to the basement to brew the sassafras into homemade root beer.

It was too complicated a recipe to follow, but it kept him busy in the basement over many nights. He poured his brew into Mason jars.

Just before daylight one February morning we were all scared out of our beds by the sound of gunfire. Ten or twelve sharp reports, like the house was surrounded.

I heard Dad's feet hit the floor in the room below me. The Hisers' bedroom light came on. We were all out of our rooms, milling.

"Dadburn it!" Grandpa barked, making for the basement in his nightshirt and Romeo bedroom shoes. The sassafras root beer had exploded, blowing the lids off all the Mason jars. Every one. How they came to go up all at once we never knew. The basement floor was awash with brown root beer, sizzling over by the furnace.

Dad was at the top of the basement stairs, bent over with his hand clapped over his mouth. Grandpa was mad as a hornet over all that work for nothing. But we were up for the day. Mom and Grandma elbowed each other out of the way, frying up eggs and our bacon ration.

The front doorbell rang, another sharp report. We stopped where we were. The spatula in Mom's hand. I raced through the house, and a kid in a delivery uniform was on the front porch in the first gray light.

It was a telegram. Another telegram, and they'd found Bill. He was alive, and safe.

We Got Bill Back . . .

. . . though he couldn't come home till after the war was over. But as Mom said, we could live with that.

In time we read his story in his V-mails. The raid over Stuttgart had been the worst one, and B-17s were knocked out of the sky all around them. Bill's crew fired their guns so fast they had to shovel the shell casings off the floor.

As bombardier, Bill sat up in the nose, and the German fighters were diving so close he could see the pilots' faces. The tail gunner was hit, and Plexiglas dust from his shattered turret blinded him. But Bill could tell him how to direct his fire, until the intercom went dead.

A 20-millimeter shell killed the waist gunner and broke the oxygen connection. They lost their place in the formation and tried for home, on their own, flying low through flak, breathing from bottles. At ten thousand feet, they saw their oil line was cut and began to bail out, hoping they were over France.

Bill came down alone in a plowed field, and the people running toward him were French Resistance fighters. They smuggled him out of sight and dressed a shoulder wound where a fragment had sliced into his flak suit.

They moved him at night from barn to barn and town to town, hiding him in farm carts, moving him nearer the coast. Then he hid in an attic in a town called Honfleur until they could get him into the hold of a fishing boat that zig-zagged on a moonless night across the Channel.

The army thawed him out and patched him up and made him an instructor, on the base Somewhere in England. They were short of instructors with all the losses.

I was through seventh grade by the time we got Bill home. But we knew that cold February morning in 1944 that we would. After a while we came to believe that Grandpa Riddle's sassafras root beers blowing up and knocking us out of bed were a twelve-gun salute to our soldier, our particular hero.

I don't know now if we ate our breakfast. I remember us in the living room, each holding the telegram in turn. It passed from Grandma's big hand with the old-fashioned wedding ring embedded in it to Mom's, and their hands brushed.

Dad held it longer, then he passed it to Grandpa and said, "Mr. Riddle, you'll get your grandson back."

Dad held Mom just for a minute before he broke away and cut off through the house, weaving because he was blinded and blurred.

He grabbed up his shotgun from behind the refrigerator, and a box of shells from under the sink. Now he was pounding off the back porch, veering out into the yard.

We watched him from the kitchen window. My dad out there barefoot in the frost in his pajamas, feeding the shells into the gun, then bringing it up to his good shoulder and firing off first one barrel, then the other.

Which was illegal within the city limits, but there were no fireworks in wartime, and Dad needed to split the sky.

I'd leave him there, my dad, feeding shells into the shotgun to wake up the world because we were getting Bill back. I'd leave him firing round after round into the leafless trees in the best morning of his life.

But he looked back at the house and waved me outside. Then I was out there with him, and he was handing me the shotgun. I felt the stock in my shoulder, and I sighted along the barrel to the bead because this was no piddly Daisy air rifle.

My head rang like a dinner bell, but I emptied both barrels into the morning, one for each of my particular heroes.